# SHADOWS
## OVER
# RAVENKIRK

1. The Last Will and Testament
of Wilhelmina Bruttenholm

### VIVIAN MOIRA VALENTINE

BLUE FORTUNE ENTERPRISES LLC

For information contact :
Blue Fortune Enterprises, LLC
Wildflower Press
P.O. Box 554
Yorktown, VA 23690
http://blue-fortune.com

Cover design by BFE, LLC

ISBN: 978-1-961548-36-7
First Edition: October 2025

dedication

*To all the monsters I've ever loved,*
*the patron saints of our blissful imperfection*

## Our Heroine and Company

*Victoria Williams*
A struggling photographer from Boston, now heir to a small fortune if she can fulfill a final request related to her hitherto before unknown mysterious parentage.

*Tina Summers*
Victoria's roommate, who is staying safely behind in Boston.

*Bianca Burke*
A private investigator hired to help Wilhelmina's research and protect Victoria.

*Samantha*
Just a tarantula.

## Wilhelmina's League

A small band of paranormal investigators based out of an occult bookstore in Ravenkirk. Famous within the occult underground, utterly unknown outside of it, which is just the way they like it.

*Wilhelmina Bruttenholm*
One of the preeminent experts on the supernatural on the Eastern seaboard, now deceased.

*Tabitha Swann*
Wilhelmina's apprentice and now de facto head of the league. An expert with the crossbow.

*Megan Ruiz*
Rough and tumble with a heart of gold, allegedly.

*Fredric Drake*
A fancy dan vampire hunter.

## Huntingdon Abbey

A not-so-secret coven of witches sworn to protect Ravenkirk from supernatural threats, both from without and within. Unfortunately, they regularly find themselves working at cross-purposes with Wilhelmina's League.

*Maledicta Harper*
Mistress of the coven and once one of Wilhelmina's greatest rivals.

*Thorn Hale*
The senior of Maledicta's apprentices, as well as the abbey's primary chef.

*Alison Thompson*
Maledicta's niece; absolutely does not mind that familial connection hasn't put her higher in the coven's hierarchy, honest.

*Tzipporah Winslow*
Gother than thou.

*Mercy Chambers*
The least friendly member of the coven, yet the abbey's primary desk clerk.

**The Ruthvens**

One of Ravenkirk's founding families. Once the most prominent family in town, the Ruthvens have fallen on hard times; that is to say, still rich but not as disgustingly so.

*Dolores Ruthven*
The family's unquestioned matriarch.

*Lavinia Ruthven*
Eldest of the youngest Ruthven generation (by six minutes).

*Basil Ruthven*
Lavinia's twin brother, who would like to be known for his own qualities, thanks.

*Nicodemus Ruthven*
The black sheep of the family, exiled about a decade ago and only now returned, to everyone's dismay.

*Belinda Pickman-Ruthven*
Youngest and most overlooked of the family.

*Montgomery Lorre*
The Ruthven family butler and last of their paid staff.

*Claude Waits*
Hereditary groundskeeper at the abandoned family manor, still hanging around for some reason.

**The Talbots**

The most prominent family of farmers and ranchers in the

surrounding countryside. No one's quite sure just how many Talbots there are, as cousins and relations come and go with surprising regularity.

*Eleanor Talbot*
Matriarch of the Talbot family.

*Hannah Talbot*
Eleanor's granddaughter and probable heir.

*George Talbot*
Hannah's younger brother.

*Hugh Talbot*
Hannah and George's cousin.

## The Gilmans

The biggest family on Ravenkirk's docks, known for their wide mouths and bulging eyes. While the Gilmans mostly keep to themselves, the town's fisherfolk follow their lead and heed their warnings.

*Patience Gilman*
Rarely seen matriarch of the Gilman family.

*Gordon Gilman*
Patience's eldest son.

*Abigail Gilman*
Patience's eldest granddaughter, who bears a particular grudge against Nicodemus Ruthven.

*Cole Gilman*
Patience's youngest grandson, although he doesn't look it.

## The Holy Association of Understanding Beyond This World

Colloquially known as the Yonders, these charming folks live on a farm outside of Ravenkirk. They occasionally come into town to spread the good word via poorly photocopied pamphlets. A cult. They're a cult.

*Waylon Earle*
The Yonders' gregarious founder and father figure.

*Jon Barlow*
Waylon's muscle.

*Eric Rutger*
Likewise Waylon's muscle.

01

The sky was the gray of old cemetery stone. Dark clouds hung above the Maine coast, threatening rain at any moment. The sun crept up the sky on schedule, but it might as well not have bothered.

To the good people of Ravenkirk, the burghers and shopkeeps and fisherfolk, the foreboding sky was barely worth mentioning. Let it hang ominously over them all it liked. It would rain or it wouldn't. Either way, there was work to be done.

*It might as well rain*, thought those in the know. Wilhelmina Bruttenholm was dead.

To say Mistress Bruttenholm was well-loved in the seaside town would be an exaggeration bordering on outright falsehood. She was a fixture of Ravenkirk's high society, a committed booster of the public library and the velvet-gloved backbone of the heritage committee. She was known but hardly liked. She was a woman who knew where the bodies were buried, and worse, where they were buried no longer.

Yet, her passing brought no one any comfort.

No, Wilhelmina Bruttenholm would not be mourned in most quarters, but she would be missed. Her passing left a hole in society, and both the natural and preternatural abhorred a vacuum. Already things were rushing to fill it.

Letters had gone out immediately upon confirmation of death, in accordance with her meticulously planned instructions. Most of them scattered across town, but some few spread down the Eastern seaboard, calling people back to Ravenkirk.

Ravenkirk simply waited, as it had for two centuries.

The morning train from Bangor hurtled down the iron rails toward the coast. It gradually sloped down through the low hills, passing through forests of dark skeletal trees and tall green conifers. Despite the lateness of the hour, a low mist clung to the ground, wrapping the landscape in mystery. The early autumn sun, hidden behind cloud cover, wasn't strong enough to banish the soft haze.

Victoria Williams didn't mind. Firstly, because she carefully cultivated the aesthetic of the sort of person who enjoyed sitting at the edge of a fog-ridden forest, all dark frilly clothes, ghost white foundation and scads of eye makeup. Secondly, because she was engrossed in the book she was reading, a thrilling tale of modern horror. That, unfortunately, wasn't enough to discourage the passenger two rows ahead of her.

"Excuse me, could I ask you a question?"

Victoria rolled her eyes in the direction of the voice. There were only so many people it could be—the passenger car held fewer than a half-dozen people. Still, its source would be unmistakable even if the train had been packed. A slender man with long, stringy dirty blond hair sat half-turned with his elbow propped on the seat. He wore a vintage floral shirt in purples and greens beneath a long dark coat and round sunglasses that would have looked more at home on John Lennon. His thin lips were twisted up into a smile.

Tension gripped Victoria's shoulders. She'd almost made it the entire trip without this. Her eyes darted to the conductor, but she expected to find little help there. Not from the way the older man had looked at her when she boarded.

She glanced at her reflection in the window. This was one of the dangers of traveling while trans. Victoria knew she was fairly clocky, even after years on hormones. Most folks understood she was female while still recognizing her as transgender. She was tall for a woman, although annoyingly still shorter than most other trans gals. Some trans women in her position tried to blend is as best they could. She'd gone the other route, embracing the Goth not-a-phase she'd been denied in high school: long black hair, absurdly complicated eye makeup, a violet mesh blouse over a black tank top, and striped leggings under black shorts.

She nodded in assent, steeling herself for what he was going to ask. Something vulgar and biological, no doubt. He seemed like the type. Her eyes darted to the conductor, but she expected to find little help there. Not from the way the older man had looked at her when she boarded. The dangers of traveling while trans.

"That book." The vulpine man pointed his sharp chin at it. "Any good?"

Victoria blinked rapidly as she forced her train of thought down a divergent track. She glanced at the cover, a young woman gazing at the sky on a field of white, black upside-down pine trees reaching from above. It was striking against the black background. The book was, in fact, pretty good. More than that, actually. She had started it when the train left Boston and was already halfway finished.

"Yes, very." She stammered over her words. "It's quite atmospheric, a mix of folk and cosmic horror. I love the characters. Jessica Conwell's an indie author; I wish she had a bigger audience."

"Hmm." He looked at the cover again. She held it up so he could get a better view. "*Ghost Flower*. Never heard of it."

Irritation creased her brow. "I *just* said—"

"I wouldn't have heard of it even if it was a bestseller." He shrugged his skinny shoulders, grin widening. "I'm not a big reader of paranormal *fiction*."

"To each their own."

Taking the conversation as over, Victoria returned to her reading. To her surprise, the slender man twisted in his seat, reaching a hand across the aisle. The bony fingers were bedecked in silver rings. His hand looked as if he'd raided a Hot Topic jewelry case.

Victoria smiled, mouth tight, and accepted his hand. It wouldn't be worth him making a scene. There was something vulpine about him, as if his too-sharp teeth might suddenly tear out her throat.

"Nicodemus Ruthven." His fingers were cool and dry, like fine sandpaper wrapped around a bundle of wooden dowels. He shook her hand exactly once, then quickly let go. He held up a warning finger. "*Just* Nicodemus. *Never* Nick or, by the powers, *Nickie*."

She nodded solemnly. "Victoria Williams. I suppose Vickie's fine. To my friends."

"I wouldn't presume." Nicodemus shifted some more, putting one foot on the seat and wrapping his arm around his knee. He wore blindingly white slacks, bright green argyle socks and scuffed dress shoes. "So, at the risk of immediately making myself a liar, what takes you to Ravenkirk?"

"Ravenkirk? What makes you think I'm going there."

"There aren't many other places to go, Ms. Williams. Unless you prefer 'Miss'?"

"Ms. is fine."

"A modern woman." That was said in a flat tone that suggested neither approval nor disappointment. "Well, you didn't get off in Bangor with everyone else. Ravenkirk isn't the end of the line, but there's hardly anything past it worth visiting. Just farmland, fishing communities, and tourist cabins, and we're well out of season." He snorted. "Granted, there's little else in Ravenkirk besides that, these days."

Victoria shifted uncomfortably in her seat. Nicodemus' green eyes pierced her, making her feel like a mouse in a corner. She glanced around for someone, anyone, to interrupt, but the other passengers were too far in the front of the car.

"Yeah, I'm going to Ravenkirk." She thought back to the black gilt-edged envelope in her roll case. "For a funeral, actually."

Nicodemus' thin eyebrows shot up. His grin grew more excited, which struck her as inappropriate. "Really? How exciting!"

He reached into his coat pocket and drew out a matching envelope. A circle of dark-red wax clung to it where he'd broken the seal. She could still make out the remains of a stylized gothic "B" stamped into the wax.

"Now, as it happens, my family is from Ravenkirk," he said as he admired the envelope. "One might say they *are* Ravenkirk. It's sort of *expected* that we'll show face. What about you? How do you know the dearly departed?"

Victoria flushed beet red. The truth was, she *didn't* know the deceased. In fact, she didn't know anyone in Ravenkirk, so far as she was aware. The invitation had arrived in the mail a week ago, informing her of Wilhelmina Bruttenholm's recent passing and notifying her of a bequest. If it hadn't been for her name clearly being marked on the envelope in white ink, she would have assumed it was a mistake. She still thought it was a misunderstanding, but she'd found herself at a loose end, and Ms. Bruttenholm's executor had assured her it would be worth her while. Victoria had figured she had nothing to lose by going. Looking into Nicodemus' green eyes, she was no longer quite so sure.

"I think she's a great-aunt or something," Victoria said, trying to sound casual.

She'd never been a great liar. Nicodemus cocked his head to the side skeptically. "'Or something'? You're not sure."

"We were never close. Not to that side of the family."

That was completely truthful. She wasn't close to either side of the family anymore. Not since she came out.

Nicodemus nodded, smile disappearing from his narrow face like a magic trick. "I know the feeling."

His mouth twitched once in an indeterminate expression. Then he turned away from her, facing the front. He slipped his thin hands into his coat pockets, shoulders hunched in a sudden sulk. For a moment, Victoria almost reached out to him. There had been something in his eyes just then, a glimmer of real emotion—pain and regret, if she wasn't mistaken. It didn't feel right to let him stew in his own estrangement. She'd certainly appreciated the friends who comforted her after Aunt Brenda said she was no longer part of the family.

Then Nicodemus started humming a jaunty tune. She didn't recognize the song; she *did* recognize the attempt to hide his feelings. Well, whatever. It wasn't her responsibility to rescue every lost stray she found, as her roommate never tired of reminding her. Especially not those who seemed likely to bite.

Grateful to be left alone, Victoria turned her attention back to her book and let the miles to Ravenkirk slide away beneath her.

"It sounds suspicious, Vickie."

Tina Summers, her roommate for the past two years, was in the kitchen washing dishes, wearing a stolen Starbucks apron over a black tank top and short shorts with a trans pride flag plastered across the ass. Despite the thrown-on messing around at home clothes, she managed to look more put together than Victoria, still dressed in her "trying for an interview" outfit. Tina might have looked like an extremely online burnout, but she was a comfortable extremely online burnout. And, thanks to her modest success at freelance graphic design, she was the one paying for rent, utilities, and groceries in their tiny apartment. Victoria knew she was a faker in her neutral makeup, beige blazer and matching pencil skirt, and so did the last five hiring managers she'd spoken to.

"That's what I thought," Victoria said, holding the black envelope out like a shield, "but I called the lawyer managing the estate. He included his card."

"Oh, well. If he included his card."

"Tina, come on. I checked his firm out. He's real."

She pulled up the website on her tablet and handed it to Tina. Her roommate didn't take her soapy hands out of the sink but amiably peered down her nose at the screen. It showed a website that had clearly been designed twenty years ago. Somehow that made it seem more legitimate. Gray, Hare and Associates weren't modern or tech savvy—the sober men in charcoal suits standing uncomfortably in front of their shingle didn't look like they had cameras in their phones, let alone Facebook—but their clients probably didn't need them to be.

Mr. Gray was well named. Somehow his voice had managed to *sound* gray even over the phone. The strange man had assured her the bequest was meant for her, Ms. Victoria Williams of Boston, Massachusetts, and that she would have to attend the will reading in person to claim it. Fortunately, the invitation had come with a train ticket and the promise of lodging.

Tina wrinkled her nose. "Where is this place?"

"About an hour southeast of Bangor."

"Never heard of it," said Tina, who'd never been north of Salem.

"I don't think it's a very big town," Victoria said. "There's not even a Wikipedia page."

Tina stared ahead, silent. She shook the soap and water from her hands, then wiped them dry on her apron. She whipped the apron over her head and hung in on its hook next to the fridge. She stared at it, hands on her hips, head shaking back and forth.

Victoria wrung her hands together. "Tina? Say something."

Tina turned slowly, her dark eyes wide. She grabbed Victoria's arm in a firm grip. "Are you sure this is safe?"

Not in the slightest. A small town in an unfamiliar area, where she didn't know anyone? Victoria wanted to blow the whole thing off. What would she find among a bunch of farmers and fishers except a cold shoulder and the risk of violence?

That wasn't enough of a deterrent.

"Maybe not, but I have to do this. What else do I have right now?"

Not any savings, that was for sure. She'd been laid off from her last job a month ago. The shitty company was struggling; the short-term solution was downsizing. Doing data entry hadn't been a calling, but it had been income. She couldn't expect Tina to keep them both afloat indefinitely.

"It's an inheritance. That probably means money. Or at least, something I can turn into money. And it'll only be for a day. Maybe two. I'll be back on Sunday."

Tina folded her arms across her chest. She wasn't convinced, but it was obvious Victoria wasn't going to be budged. It wasn't like her to stand in Victoria's way.

"You call me as soon as you get there," she said. "You call me and you be safe."

As the train hurtled ever closer to its destination, it took a sharp turn to the north. Approaching the coast, it emerged from the dark woods, giving Victoria her first look at Ravenkirk. It was a small town, nestled between low hills to the north and the crinkly coastline to the south. Most of the dark buildings looked vintage: Colonial, Gothic Revival, Edwardian. This town had never erupted in the beige rectangles symptomatic of the strip mall infection. The local historical society must be working overtime here.

Nicodemus perked up as the town rushed toward them. He

rose from his seat, clearly trying to appear casual, and leaned against the window. The trembling of his bony fingers against the glass gave him away.

"What's got you so excited?" Victoria asked despite herself.

Nicodemus looked back over his shoulder, sheepish. "It's been a long time since I've been … home."

"Oh." Victoria felt a sharp pang of jealousy. Must be nice, being able to go home. Guilt nipped at jealousy's heels. It wasn't Nicodemus' fault. "I'm glad for you."

Nicodemus stared at her, eyes blinking rapidly. He tilted his head to one side, as if he was trying to process that. "Thank you?"

Ravenkirk rapidly grew from a toy village to a full-grown settlement as the train rushed down the hill. Nicodemus tapped the glass when a long building with a green and white striped awning rushed past.

"It's still open!" He sounded like a schoolboy minutes before the last bell of the year. "Sal's Sandwich Shoppe! That was my favorite place to eat when I was a teenager."

Victoria nodded politely. "I'll have to check it out, if I have time."

"You should. They do a hell of a lobster roll." He grinned, somewhat nastily. "Much cheaper than you'll get in *Bah*-ston."

That did sound appealing, though she didn't want to admit it. Lodging for the night had been provided, not meals. "I never said I was from Boston."

"Yes, you did. Every time you tried to pronounce an 'R'."

"I …" Victoria stood, drawing herself up to her full height—a good six inches above Nicodemus—and adopted the worst Maine accent she could muster. "Waal, it's a long way from theya, but ah reckon I made it all right, ayuh."

Nicodemus scowled. "I sound nothing like that."

"Nah dun't get yuh drawas in a twist, nah."

"You are a fool, and I retract my recommendation. You don't deserve Sal's lobster rolls."

Victoria shrugged, nonplussed. "I hear you folks eat them cold anyway."

Nicodemus sat down, deliberately turning his back to her. Victoria suppressed a giggle and returned to her own seat as the train slid into the station. Hopefully this was the last she would have to deal with him. His moods were too unpredictable.

## 02

To Victoria's surprise, another woman was waiting for her at the station. She was a tall Black woman wearing a red button-up and gray slacks beneath a long charcoal-gray coat with burgundy lining, carrying a hand-written sign with Victoria's name on it. Her skin was a deep brown, except for pale patches of vitiligo around her mouth and right eye, and her dark hair floated around her in a gorgeous twist-out. She smiled when her eyes met Victoria's, shaking the sign as a question.

"Um, hi!" Victoria said, trotting quickly across the platform to greet her. "I wasn't expecting someone to be waiting for me."

"We didn't want you getting lost." The other woman offered her hand. "Tabitha Swann."

Victoria took Tabitha's hand. The other woman smiled brightly, shooting a jolt through Victoria's breast. She found herself staring into Tabitha's dark eyes.

*Oh no*, she thought. *She's so pretty.*

"Victoria Williams," she stammered. Tabitha's grip was strong, her fingers smooth and warm. Victoria resisted the urge to rub her thumb over the back of Tabitha's hand. "Um. Obviously. Or else I wouldn't be who you were waiting for."

"I'm certainly glad you are." Tabitha dropped her hand, leaving Victoria with a brief pang of regret. "For a while there, we were afraid you weren't coming."

"Oh, I wouldn't have missed it!" Victoria laughed awkwardly, trying to ignore the burning in her cheeks. "A charming town like this? Who wouldn't want to visit?"

Tabitha glanced around the open-air train station, a quizzical look on her face. The metal awning holding up the slate roof did nothing to hide the dark buildings around the station. Up close, they were far more run-down than Victoria had realized. The paint was peeling, the roofs missing shingles, and the cobblestoned streets missing stones. A chill mist clung to the ground, even this late in the morning. The people trudging along the sidewalks seemed not to notice, although it was hard to tell beneath their typical New England dourness.

"I wouldn't call this place 'charming', exactly," Tabitha said. "Atmospheric, certainly."

"It's a dump that smells unrepentantly of fish," Nicodemus said from behind them. "Hello, Tabitha. Think you'll finally escape now that the old bat's dead?"

Tabitha rolled her eyes at the sneering man and sighed heavily. "Nicodemus. I wasn't expecting to see you."

Victoria looked over her shoulder at Nicodemus, then back to Tabitha. The obvious hostility between them made her tense up. She suddenly wanted to be anywhere else, but there was nowhere to flee to. Instead, she drew her lips up into a defensive almost-smile.

"I take it you two know each other?"

"In a town this small?" Nicodemus' smile widened, exposing his sharp teeth. "Everyone knows everyone."

"We know *of* each other." Tabitha gave him a condescending look. "Nickie's been *persona non grata* in Ravenkirk for over a decade."

"A misunderstanding." He pulled the black envelope out of his coat pocket. "I'm quite welcome now."

"For the weekend." Tabitha crossed her arms. "Stay out of trouble, Nicodemus."

"I *always* avoid trouble. It just has a habit of seeking me out." He pocketed the invitation and walked away, giving them a jaunty wave. "See you at the reading. I'm sure it'll be the social event of the season."

"What an ass," Tabitha said to Nicodemus' back, but too quietly for him to hear.

"He was friendly on the train," Victoria said. "I mean, like a stray cat who hadn't decided whether to scratch."

"That's a good description. Stay away from him if you can."

Tabitha led Victoria out of the station and to her truck, parked along the street—not a massive pavement monster, but a compact pickup that had to be at least twenty years old. It was deep red under the dirt, and a gray canvas tarp covered whatever lumpy load filled its bed. Victoria went to put her roll case in the bed, but Tabitha stopped her.

"Here, let me. It's, ah, kind of a mess back there." She laughed awkwardly. "Sorry, didn't plan ahead, I guess. I know where it'll fit."

Victoria let Tabitha take her small suitcase and tuck it into the bed. It took ten minutes—increasingly frustrating for Tabitha, increasingly awkward for Victoria—but eventually the case was stowed and the tarp tied down. Tabitha gave her a bright smile.

"Ready to go?"

"Yeah." They climbed into the truck. "Where am I staying, anyway?"

"Nice little place on the north side of town. Actually, let me call ahead real quick and make sure your room is ready."

Tabitha reached into her coat pocket for her phone and let out a surprised shriek. She yanked her hand out, sending the phone clattering onto the footwell and a large black tarantula flying across the cab. The hairy spider landed on the dashboard and skittered around, clearly agitated.

"Oh my God!" Victoria said. "Are you okay?"

"I'm fine." Tabitha glanced at her hand. It was unmarked. "She didn't bite me. Fucking Ruthvens."

Victoria glanced at the side mirror. Nicodemus Ruthven was reflected in it, grinning nastily. She turned around to yell at him through the rear window, but he was nowhere to be seen. When she looked back, his reflection had likewise disappeared.

"How'd he get such a big spider in your pocket? Where did she come from?"

"He's tricky. Like I said, stay away from him."

The tarantula huddled in the left corner between the dashboard and the windshield. She was striking, with white stripes down her legs and an oblong white smudge on the top of her abdomen. Victoria felt a pang of sympathy.

"Poor thing. She's probably more scared of us."

"Yeah." Tabitha gave the spider an appraising look. "I guess it's not your fault, huh?"

Telling Victoria to hold on, Tabitha hopped back out of the truck and dug around under the canvas tarp. After a few moments, she emerged with a heavy cardboard shoe box. She poked a half-dozen holes in the lid with her keys. Then Victoria coaxed the spider into the box.

"That should do for now." Tabitha turned on the engine and pulled out into the street. "You'll want to get your new friend a better enclosure soon."

"Oh, I'm not keeping her." Victoria laughed. "I just want her to be safe until we find somewhere to let her out."

Tabitha gave her a look. "You sure about that? This isn't the climate for that sort of critter, especially since it's just going to get colder."

"Oh." Victoria sat quietly for a minute, holding the box in her lap. She imagined the tarantula inside looking at her plaintively. "Well, we'll figure something out."

"Shit, that reminds me." Tabitha grabbed her phone to make

a call. "Hey, Mercy, it's Tabitha. Tabitha Swann." She glanced at Victoria and rolled her eyes. "We met in elementary school, Mercy, you know who I am. I've got Ms. Williams. I'm just checking to see if her room is ready. Okay, cool. Well, I'm very sorry to have made you do your job."

Tabitha hung up and dropped her phone on the seat between them. "Asshole."

"Is something wrong?" Victoria said, hesitantly.

"Not a thing, honey." Tabitha gave her a warm smile. "Your room is ready for you. You can get settled as soon as we're there. It's a nice place, but today's manager is a pain in the ass."

"Cool. Did you arrange this?"

"Not exactly. I worked for Wilhelmina, but Mr. Gray is the executor of her estate. He arranged everything."

"I still appreciate you picking me up."

"It's no problem." Tabitha gave her knee a quick squeeze, starting a warm flush in Victoria's belly. "I liked meeting you."

Victoria ducked her head to hide her blush. Tabitha liked meeting her! That probably didn't mean anything, but it made her happy to hear all the same. Then she felt a sudden pang of guilt. She had to come clean before she got in too deep.

"Tabitha? I need to confess something."

"What? Were you the one who slipped the spider in my coat?"

"No, no!" Victoria laughed despite herself. "The thing is, I don't know Wilhelmina Bruttenholm at all. I think there's been a mistake."

Tabitha nodded. "I can tell."

"What? How?"

"Because her name's pronounced 'Brüm'." Tabitha grinned. "There's no mistake. Mr. Gray was very thorough. So was Wilhelmina. You might not have known who she was, but she knew who you were. If she left you something, it was for a reason."

If that was meant to be reassuring, it failed. Victoria sat silently for the rest of the ride. It wasn't long, since Ravenkirk wasn't a large town. Tabitha took them north along the gently curving Main Street until they came to a low hill at the edge of town. A long, narrow building in Jacobethan style sat atop it, built of gray and black brick. A gravel parking lot spread around the foot of the hill, where a sign named it "Huntingdon Abbey" in looping script.

"An abbey?" Victoria asked.

"Not for a long time. It's a boarding house now. Has been for, oh, fifty, sixty years? This is where Mr. Gray put you up." Her voice carried a hint of "for some reason".

Over Victoria's half-hearted objection, Tabitha grabbed her roll case out of the truck and took it up the path to the front steps. A wrought-iron knocker was affixed to the antique wooden door, a raven's head over two spread wings. It held the iron ring in its beak. Tabitha knocked twice, then stepped back, arms folded across her chest. Her lips twitched. After a moment, Victoria realized she was counting under her breath.

At fifty-seven, the door creaked open. A petite woman in a long white sweater and short, black-and-blue checked skirt stood in the doorway. Her blonde hair was cut in a messy bob and streaked with pink and purple. Three silver chains hung from her neck, each holding a witchy pendant.

"Welcome to Huntingdon Abbey," she said to Victoria, sounding bored. Her kohl-rimmed eyes cut to Tabitha. "What do you want, Tabby?"

Tabitha took a deep breath and fixed something not unlike a smile to her face. "I have a check-in for you, Mercy. The one we just spoke about over the phone? This is Ms. Williams."

Mercy's eyes briefly widened as they cut back to Victoria. Feeling a sudden wave of self-consciousness, Victoria hugged the shoe box to her chest as if she might hide behind it. Mercy had figured out something about her. It was just a question of what, and how she would react.

The unfriendly woman widened her mouth at Victoria, holding out her arms in a nearly welcoming gesture. "Come right in, Ms. Williams. Your room's ready for you." The not-quite-smile dropped when she looked back to Tabitha. "I guess you can come in, too."

"You're too kind." Tabitha gestured for Victoria to go inside, then followed her.

The front room took up the whole width of the building. The floors were hardwood, the walls painted deep blue with dark wood wainscotting. A heavy wooden desk sat against the far wall, next to an open doorway leading to a long hallway. A portrait in a silver frame hung above the desk. It depicted a handsome older woman in a midnight blue dress, her dark red hair sculpted into a bouffant. She wore a heavy silver ring on one hand, sporting a large oval-cut amber in a scrollwork setting. The signature, a messy scrawl in which only the initials "V" and "P" were legible, dated to portrait to either 1988 or 1888.

Mercy struck a pose, adopting a tour guide persona. "Welcome to historic Huntingdon Abbey. Formerly a convent for a congregation of Carmelite nuns, local eccentric Howard Huntingdon purchased the property in 1925 after they disbanded. The current owner, Mistress Harper, inherited the property in 1974 after his death, whereupon she converted it into a boarding house."

Mercy gestured to the portrait, evidently of Mistress Harper. She then led them down the long hallway, their footsteps echoing on the hardwood floors.

"Although the abbey has been periodically renovated and modernized, you'll find it retains all the *fin-de-siècle* charm and atmosphere guests know and love. The main dining hall is here on the first floor. We serve a complimentary breakfast and dinner; you can find the week's menu posted in the drawing room. You are, of course, welcome to eat on your own in your room, but our rooms do not come with refrigerators, and hot plates and the like aren't permitted. Each floor shares a bathroom, so please be considerate of your fellow guests. We don't have satellite, cable or Wi-Fi, but the library is well-stocked with books and a wide selection of something called VHS tapes."

"Oh, I don't think that will be relevant." Victoria laughed awkwardly. Mercy gave her a sharp look. "I'm only staying for one night. For Ms. Bruttenholm's will reading."

Mercy stood with her hands on her hips, lip curled. "Well, aren't you in luck? The will reading's being held *here* in the drawing room, so you'll need to know where that is." She gestured to the door on the right. "It's through this door. Dining room's across the hall to your left, in case you decide to eat tonight. Library's the next door down on *this* side, adjoining the drawing room. Kitchen's the next door down on *that* side, adjoining the dining room, and it's off-limits to guests. Stairs are at the far end of this hall. You're on the top floor. Will you be waiting downstairs, Tabby?" Mercy smiled nastily. "You know Mistress Harper has *rules* about visitors in the rooms."

Victoria cringed in embarrassment, but Tabitha waved her off. She rolled her eyes and passed Victoria the handle of her roll case. Victoria ducked her head sheepishly, then followed Mercy down the hall and up both flights of stairs, shoebox tucked under her arm. The ceiling on the top floor was lower than the other two levels, practically an attic. Like the first floor, a single long hallway ran its length, with six doors on either side.

"You're in 303." Mercy handed her the room key. "Bathroom's the third door on the right, linen closet's the third door on the left. Dinner's at six, the reading's at eight. If you have any questions, please don't hesitate to get lost."

Victoria opened her mouth to ask one, then realized what Mercy had said. The rude woman turned to go. Victoria went to her room, then decided she was going to ask anyway.

"What, um, what *are* the rules about visitors in the rooms?"

Mercy looked over her shoulder and shrugged. "Thought you weren't going to be here long enough for it to matter?"

Well, that was Victoria told. She scowled at Mercy's retreating form, then unlocked her room. To say it was Spartan was overselling it. There were three pieces of furniture—a twin-sized bed on a metal frame, a short dresser, and a wooden chair.

*At least there's a window*, she thought.

She sat the shoebox on top of the dresser and rolled her suitcase next to it. No sense in unpacking. She only had the two changes of clothes, anyway—a clean shirt and jeans for traveling and a nice dress for the reading. It seemed like something she ought to dress up for.

Victoria sat down on the bed, hearing the metal springs squeak in protest, and wondered what she'd gotten herself into. She didn't have long to ponder before her phone buzzed. It was a text message.

"Hey, it's Tabitha. There's someone down here to see you."

## 03

The Ruthven family estate sat atop a low hill on Mockingbird Lane, in Ravenkirk's well-to-do west side. Frankly, calling it an "estate" was putting on airs, in Nicodemus' not at all humble opinion. The *true* family estate was outside the town proper, on the Eveningwood Ridge, overlooking the people who rightfully belonged to them. This was practically a McMansion, dodging that appellation only by its adherence to Ravenkirk's strict architectural standards, thank the Heritage Committee. The result was an unholy marriage of Queen Anne and Craftsman. By rights, it ought to be a townhouse, narrowly escaping that fate by a fifteen-foot gap between neighbors on either side.

"Shameful," Nicodemus said, looking up at a house that would sell for nearly two million dollars on the current market. "How far we have fallen."

He swung open the wrought-iron gate and strode up the stone

steps, dark coat billowing behind him. The gold velvet curtains in a second-floor window twitched. He caught a brief glimpse of cornsilk-blonde hair and grinned. It was good to have an audience.

The house had a doorbell, but that wouldn't do. He grabbed the iron doorknocker, held in a goat's mouth, and rapped thrice. The sound echoed through the front room. He took a step back on the porch and waited, hands in his coat pockets and hips cocked insolently. It took five minutes for someone to answer the door; that did nothing to harm his malignant humor.

The door creaked open a precisely measured ten inches. A bent, slight man in his fifties stood with a dour expression. He wore a butler's livery—a dark coat with tails over a gold waistcoat—and his sparse hair and moustache were shot with gray. He glowered at Nicodemus as if he was an unwanted solicitor.

"How may I help you?" he asked in a reedy voice.

"Monty, old boy! You're still breathing?" Nicodemus grabbed the door and pushed it open, ignoring the butler's weak protest. "Are you telling me you don't recognize me? Your mind can't be *that* bad yet."

The butler withdrew a painstakingly polished set of pince-nez from his coat and peered through them. His scowl deepened as they confirmed what he already knew. Montgomery Lorre knew him, indeed; he'd served the Ruthven family faithfully for more than forty years, from footman to valet to finally succeeding his father as butler after the old man's unfortunate death. He'd known Nicodemus as a boy and as a young man and detested him as both. He wanted nothing more than for the prodigal Ruthven to *not* be darkening the family's doorstep, yet there was no such luck.

"Master Nicodemus," he wheezed. "You were not expected."

"Not expected? In my own home? Why, Monty, I'm hurt!"

Lorre sniffed fastidiously. "This is *not* your home."

Nicodemus didn't disagree. He had never lived in this building. The family had descended to this state well after he'd been exiled from Ravenkirk. Nonetheless, this was the Ruthven family estate, and he was a Ruthven.

"You can argue that, Monty. You really can." Nicodemus leaned forward until his head had crossed the threshold, grinning dangerously. "I don't think my dear auntie would see it the same way, do you? Do you want to risk it?"

To his credit, the butler didn't step back from the doorway. He couldn't help but lean away, though, eyes darting back and forth as he considered his options. Dolores Ruthven was the unquestioned head of the family. She was the one who dictated that the family estate be open to all Ruthvens, even the most disreputable. Yet, she had also voted in favor of Nicodemus' banishment, after his antics had grown too much for the best of Ravenkirk to bear. A bead of oily sweat dripped down Lorre's brow. What would she say now?

"You can go ask, of course," Nicodemus said. "It'd make you look weak, though. And I'd just follow you inside anyway, so what's the point, eh?"

A wheedling whine escaped Lorre's lips, and his grip on the door tightened. Ruthvens didn't train their help to defy their orders. Neither had they traditionally had much pity when those orders conflicted.

Lorre's salvation came when a blandly handsome voice called from down the hall. "Hell's bells, is that Cousin Nicky?"

Nicodemus' grin disappeared for just a moment. He plastered it back when the other man came into view. His elder cousin, Basil Ruthven, a blond man with a sportsman's build and a banker's heart. He wore his letterman's sweater from Collinswood Academy, the private school they'd all attended, because of course he still did. Nicodemus had to admit that it still fit, even in Basil's mid-thirties.

"It is indeed Master Nicodemus," Lorre said sadly.

"Course it is. Who else would it be?" Nicodemus leaned against the door jamb. "You look well, Basil. That moustache isn't stupid at all."

Basil brushed at the hair on his lip, self-conscious. "Uh. Thanks. I take it you're back for the, um…"

"For the 'um', indeed, Basil. You've such a way with words. I've always said that."

The butler shifted uncomfortably. "Master Basil, Mistress Ruthven was quite clear…"

"Aunt Dolores has been clear about a lot of things, Lorre. He's still family. Let him in."

"There, see? Problem solved. Now it's Basil's fault." Nicodemus pushed through the door. "You gonna get out of my way now, Monty?"

"My apologies, Master Nicodemus." Lorre's reedy voice was entirely insincere. "May I get you anything?"

"A club sandwich would be nice. Don't skimp on the bacon.

They didn't have meal service on the train, can you believe that?"

Lorre glanced at Basil, who nodded once. "Come on, Nickie. Let me show you around."

"Oh, please do." Nicodemus smirked. "I'm *dying* for a tour."

Basil's face fell, a slow-motion avalanche as bland friendliness was overtaken by tired irritation. Nicodemus delighted to see such a light barb stung him so easily. Basil wasn't a threat. He wasn't even an obstacle. He was just *there*, a boring backup to Auntie's plans, albeit one more likely to produce a next generation than most other available candidates.

"Perhaps we ought to just go tell Aunt Dolores you're here," he muttered into his moustache.

"Don't bother. Monty isn't making me a sandwich." Nicodemus pushed past him, hands folded behind his back as he pretended to admire the décor. "He's already scurried ahead to tattle on me." He tossed a look over his shoulder. "Well, us. You're the one who let the prodigal cousin in without asking."

Basil harumphed. "So it's going to be like that, then?"

"Same as it ever was, dear cousin. Haven't you missed me?"

Basil's handsome face went red. He balled his fists as if he might strike. Nicodemus only smiled wider. He wouldn't dare. No fighting between the family, not in the family home. Aunt Dolores wouldn't have it. Even without fear of her disapproval, though, Basil wouldn't strike at Nicodemus. Not directly, and he wasn't the sort to be indirect. He might have inherited all the athleticism, but Nicodemus had the art.

A portrait hung at the end of the front hall, nearly life-sized.

It depicted a tall, handsome woman in a dark gown. A glittering ruby cameo sat at her throat, held there by a black silk choker. She wore a silver ring, but its setting was empty. The ghost of a three-masted sailing ship plied the waves over her shoulder—a memory of the family's crossing over the Atlantic, he supposed. The woman's pinched face, surrounded by a crown of iron-gray hair, glared imperiously down at the viewer. Old Pickman had captured Dolores Ruthven's likeness pretty well.

"How is dear old Auntie D?" Nicodemus asked amiably.

"You can ask her yourself," said a high-pitched voice.

Nicodemus turned to see a slender teenage girl standing in the doorway to the drawing room, one hand on her hip. Her ash-blonde hair fell past her shoulders. She wore gold silk pajamas festooned with white blossoms. Her face had the Ruthven features—high cheekbones, a narrow chin, an air of unearned superiority—but Nicodemus couldn't place her. Guessing at her age, he took a stab in the dark.

"Little Belinda? My, how you've grown!"

Belinda Pickman-Ruthven didn't look mollified at all by his recognition. She cocked her hip to the side and crossed her arms, looking at him as if he was a bug about to be pinned. He liked her already.

"You left." Her voice carried unmistakable accusation.

He remembered her as a young girl, running after him as he explored the family cemetery, dancing in the tall grass on Sentinel Hill, performing amateur surgery on a series of stuffies. She used to sit for hours listening to his stories about the family history, about his latest discoveries, about the things that went bump in the night. She'd been fierce and fearless. He hoped she'd stayed that way, instead of settling for being the terror of the Collinswood Academy social set.

"I'm sorry, Belle." He walked forward, holding his arms out. "They made me leave."

Her glare permitted no excuses. "You didn't even say goodbye."

"They didn't give me the chance." Nicodemus put his finger beneath her chin, tilting her face up. "Do you really think I would have left by favorite cousin behind on anything short of the pain of death?"

She glared up at him for a moment longer, her eyes chips of emerald ice. Then they thawed under the excitement of seeing him again. Belinda threw her arms around him, burying her face in his silk shirt.

"Oh, *Nickie!*" she cried. "You've come home!"

Nicodemus hugged her back, pressing his sharp cheek to the top of her head. "They couldn't keep me away for long, little flower."

"More's the pity," said another voice from inside the drawing room.

Nicodemus and Belinda turned to face the newcomer, still embracing. A tall woman descended the stairs on the drawing room's west wall. She wore a gold tunic and black-and-white checked slacks. A red gem clung to the white choker around her throat, but it wasn't the one in Dolores' portrait; Nicodemus was certain it wasn't even a real ruby. Her cornsilk-blonde hair had been chopped in a butch cut that surely drove Dolores mad. Nicodemus could respect that, if nothing else about her.

"Dear Lavinia," he said. "How nice to see you again."

Lavinia Ruthven, Basil's twin and the eldest of the current Ruthven generation, simply curled her lip in response. She crossed the room and took a seat on the couch against the east wall. The others took that as their cue to enter the drawing room. A baroque chair, dark wood upholstered in deep gold, dominated the room. None of them dared to sit in it. Basil sat in the corner, across the room from his sister. Belinda sat on the floor at Lavinia's feet, giving Nicodemus an apologetic look. Nicodemus preferred to stand, taking a place in the center of the room, turning back and forth to smile at his cousins like a shark.

"Well. The gang's all here." Basil coughed into his fist. "I suppose we have a lot to catch up on."

"Do we?" Lavinia asked, glaring at Nicodemus.

"Wait. This is everyone?" Nicodemus looked around the room. "Really?"

Basil looked uncomfortable. "The family's suffered a lot of misfortune since you, ah, moved away."

"I wonder how that could have happened," Lavinia said angrily.

Nicodemus rolled his eyes. "I couldn't possibly say, as I was on the other coast for the past decade. Where are the old ones?"

"Your daddy died six years ago," Lavinia said with a smirk. "Were you not informed?"

"I received the letter a month after the funeral," Nicodemus said, unbothered. "A shame. I would have liked to have gone, although I suppose I still have time to defile his grave."

"You're grotesque, Nickie." Basil shook his head. "Uncle Ezekiel was the last of his generation. Our parents died before you left, remember?"

"Mother died birthing me," Belinda said cheerfully. "Daddy ran off not long after."

"Uncle Saul's still in the asylum." Lavinia paused. "Wait, was that before you were run off or after?"

"Both, I think," Basil said.

Nicodemus tried to recall the names of the other cousins. There were so many. "What happened to Josephine?"

"Went boating and drowned in the bay," Lavinia said.

"Jeremiah?"

"Hunting accident!" Belinda said.

"The other twins? Hamish and Hannah?"

"Hamish drove his car off a cliff while blind drunk. Hannah ran away after the funeral and hasn't been seen since."

"Tristram?"

"Hung himself, the poor fellow."

"The, ah, the ugly one with the mole?"

"You mean our younger brother Isaac." Lavinia's voice was cold as ice.

"That's the one. How's he?"

Basil looked down at his feet. "We're not sure. He disappeared five years ago. Mysterious circumstances."

"I don't know what to say." Nicodemus shook his head. "You

certainly have been careless with your family members in my absence."

"There's been a lot of that going around." Lavinia fixed him with a cold look. "You know what happened to Enoch."

Nicodemus' expression curdled into a fearsome scowl. "I know full well what happened to my brother."

Lavinia smiled cruelly. "Yes, I thought you might. That's what started *your* whole mess, isn't it?"

"*I* don't know what happened to Cousin Enoch." Belinda pouted. "No one tells me anything."

"It's not a story for your ears, pet," Lavinia cooed, stroking Belinda's hair. "You'll hear it when you're older."

"I'm not a child, *Lavinia*."

"An outburst like that suggests otherwise."

The cousins' bickering died in their throats. All looked up to the tall woman at the landing. Nicodemus forced himself to smile, baring sharp teeth.

"Auntie Dolores! So wonderful to see you."

"Nicodemus."

Dolores Ruthven descended the stairs, one hand holding the skirt of her white gown. Despite his disdain for her, Nicodemus couldn't help but admire her commitment to her aesthetic. No pantsuits, robes or athleisurewear for her. Even with the family fortunes dwindled to next to nothing, the head of the Ruthven family still comported herself as if she was to attend a formal occasion at any moment.

Which, to be fair, she would tonight.

Lorre appeared at the foot of the stairs, carrying a silver tray. It held a crystal glass of white wine and not, as Nicodemus had predicted, his club sandwich. Dolores took the offered drink without looking at her butler; by his proud expression, he expected nothing less. Her attention was focused entirely on her wayward nephew. A decade ago, he would have wilted under her gaze, averting his eyes, stammering out a wheedling apology. Not now. Nicodemus stared back, eyes meeting hers, grin just a touch below outright insolence.

"I thought you knew what 'banished' meant," Dolores said.

"It was the first thing all the families agreed on in decades," Lavinia added.

"I love the way I bring people together." Nicodemus produced his invitation, gilt edges gleaming in the light. "Much like a funeral. I assume I'll see you there, dear auntie?"

Dolores slowly lowered herself into the baroque chair, one elbow propped up on an arm. Nicodemus knew it well, even if he hadn't seen it in this room before. He'd stood before her many times as a child, sitting in this chair and staring imperiously down at him as she did now, his own weak-willed father cringing in the hallway. Ezekiel Ruthven never meted out discipline. That was for Dolores and Dolores alone.

Well, Nicodemus Ruthven was not his father. Nor was he his cousins, scurrying at their great-aunt's heels seeking a scrap of approval. He was the last true Ruthven, and he needed no one's approval.

"I was surprised to hear the old bat had passed on. I thought

Wilhelmina would never go. Shove over, Lavinia." Nicodemus sat in the middle of the couch, forcing Lavinia to slide sideways. Belinda shifted surreptitiously, until she sat between them. "How'd you kill her, auntie?"

"That's a disgusting accusation!" Basil said, rage screwing up his ridiculously boring lacrosse player's face. "Mistress Bruttenholm passed quietly in her study. There hasn't been the slightest suggestion of foul play."

"Yes, Basil, because that's how people like us die." Nicodemus spoke to his older cousin as if he was a child. "We get tired of poking our noses where they don't belong and keel over quietly in our comfy chairs. Out with it, Aunt Dolores. I want to know the game before I play."

Dolores took a casual sip of wine. "Wilhelmina died of natural causes, so far as anyone knows. She *was* an old woman."

"Yeah, that's why I blame you." Nicodemus raised a hand and began counting off on long fingers. "It wasn't messy enough to be the Talbots. The Gilmans like the water; you'd never have found a body. Maledicta's lost her edge, though she doesn't want to admit it, and I doubt any of her girls have the stuff. Can't be the newcomers. The Claremonts don't have it in 'em— they'll foreclose on your house, not cut your throat—and those bumpkins in the hills have the subtlety of a thrown brick."

Dolores gave him an appraising look. "You've been keeping up with events."

"I try to stay abreast, Auntie dear." Nicodemus spread his arms wide. "That just leaves the family. Basil doesn't have what it takes—no offense, cuz—Lavinia isn't good enough, no matter what she thinks, and I've been out of town." He leaned forward, a foxlike grin on his narrow face. "How'd you do it, Auntie? Professional curiosity."

"You left out Belinda," Lavinia murmured.

Nicodemus glanced down at their younger cousin. She looked back at him, green eyes wide. Her brow furrowed in confusion. Obviously, it wasn't her.

"Don't be vulgar, Lavinia." Nicodemus sniffed.

Dolores set her empty wine glass on the table next to her. "I didn't kill her, Nicodemus. I don't believe anyone else did, either. As shocking as this might sound to you, sometimes people just die."

"Not when Nicodemus is around." Lavinia scowled at him. "Then there's always a culprit."

"I won't apologize for being efficient." Nicodemus stood. "Well, this went as well as could be expected. Since you won't be honest with me, I suppose I'll see myself out."

"Don't be absurd." Dolores sniffed. "Where are your things? Lorre will take them up to your room."

"I don't *have* a room here," Nicodemus said.

"You're a Ruthven. You *all* have a room here."

"And yet. You can wipe that sour look off your face, Monty. I won't be staying in this monument to family decay." Nicodemus turned to leave, ignoring Belinda's protests.

Dolores rose to her feet, a trifle unsteadily. "I didn't say you were dismissed, boy."

"I didn't ask."

"Oh, don't be petulant, Nicky." Lavinia rolled her eyes. "Where else would you stay?"

"Not at the Abbey," Basil said, smug. "Maledicta wouldn't have him."

"My accommodations are my own affair," Nicodemus said, "as is my business here. See you at the reading tonight; don't sit next to me."

Basil spluttered as Nicodemus left the study. Belinda started to cry, while Lavinia said something arch that he didn't bother to catch. Dolores just stared at him. She couldn't do anything else.

She had no power. That was the lesson he'd learned in his exile. Nicodemus knew where the true power in Ravenkirk was locked away. He just needed the key.

## 04

Victoria couldn't guess who was waiting for her downstairs in this town full of strange people, but had she tried, she never would have predicted Bianca Burke.

A third woman had joined Tabitha and Mercy in the lobby. Both of them eyed her with wariness. A short woman in her late thirties, she wore a leather jacket over a tight white jumpsuit, her ice-white hair done up in a slick bun. She smiled when she saw Victoria, indifferent to the glances Mercy and Tabitha threw her.

"There's my detail." She held out a hand with short-trimmed nails. "Bianca Burke, private investigator."

A twinned chill and thrill ran up Victoria's arm. Bianca's hand was firm, with the exciting calluses of rough work. Victoria wanted to know more about that work. She also felt a sudden wave of guilt for no reason she could say.

"Who… what are you investigating?" she stammered.

Bianca grinned. "You, actually."

"Wilhelmina hired Ms. Burke to look you up," Tabitha said. "She didn't say why."

"You'll find out at the will reading," Bianca said. "My job was to find you and get you there. I was supposed to pick you up in Boston, actually, but that lawyer muttered something about 'billable hours' and bought a train ticket instead."

"I didn't mind," Victoria said. "I liked the train ride."

"You'd like riding with me better." The way Bianca winked ought to have been a crime in most jurisdictions. "That's why I'm here, besides checking up on you. If you want to get out and see the town, I'll take you wherever you want to go."

"Mistress Harper is guaranteeing your safety while you're within the abbey walls," Tabitha said. "Ms. Burke's assignment is to shadow you when you're not here. Apparently."

"I see," said Victoria, who didn't. "Am I in some sort of danger that I should know about?"

"No!" Tabitha said, as Bianca said, "Not exactly."

Mercy rolled her eyes. "Why would a boring little nobody like *you* be in danger?"

"There's that hospitality that's earned the abbey over a hundred one-star reviews," Tabitha said.

"Fuck off, Tabby."

"*Ladies.*"

Bianca's voice was mild, but it brooked no disagreement. Both women backed down. What was clearly an old grudge still simmered between them like August air above a sidewalk, but they resolved to ignore one another. Since escalation was no longer imminent, Bianca dismissed them.

"So, that's the deal," Bianca said. "If you just want to hang out in your room until evening, I can kick rocks and attend to the rest of my duties. Or we can go for a ride. The choice is entirely up to you, ladybug."

"Whatever gets you all out of my lobby the quickest," Mercy grumbled.

Victoria looked from Bianca to Tabitha. Of the two, she'd much rather go out with Tabitha. On the town, that is. Bianca was certainly exciting—something about the way she moved suggested well-developed muscles beneath her clothes—but Tabitha seemed more like Victoria's type. As if that was something she could tell after knowing a woman for less than an hour.

"Tabitha?" she said hesitantly. "Would you like to come with us?"

Tabitha's apologetic expression seemed genuine. "I wish I could, but I have to get to work. I'll see you at the will reading, though."

Mercy muttered something too low for the others to hear. Ignoring her, Tabitha took Victoria by the arm, just above her elbow. Victoria tingled where she touched.

"I do hope we have a chance to hang out before you go," Tabitha said.

Victoria blushed. "I'd like that. A lot."

Bianca shook her head, but she was grinning. "Glad that's settled. How about it, ladybug?"

"Sure," Victoria said. "I suppose I have plenty of time."

"Nothing but. Come on, I'm parked out front."

"And technically I can't leave until she moves," Tabitha added.

Bianca's car was parked across the middle of the gravel lot. Victoria didn't know anything about cars, but she knew it was fast and expensive. Somehow it was blindingly white despite the gray, muddy day.

Bianca slipped on a pair of round shades—unnecessary, considering the weather, but still impossibly cool. "Hop in. I'll take you wherever s'long as it's in town."

"Thanks." Victoria hesitated. "Kind of a lot for a daily driver, isn't it?"

"The job takes me all over the place. I like to get there in style. You coming or what?"

Victoria climbed into the passenger seat. Bianca waited until she was buckled, then threw the car into reverse, whipping around in what might have been a zero-point turn. The white car peeled out of the parking lot, spraying mud and gravel in its wake.

"So, ladybug, where to?"

"Pardon?"

"Where do you want to go? Grocery shopping, sight-seeing, fishing on the pier? I do not recommend that last one. You're not dressed for it and they pull all sorts of crap out of that bay."

"Um." Victoria stared at her. "I don't really know anything about this place. I guess lunch? I'm kind of hungry."

"Lunch it is. Local or chain?"

"Not Sal's Sandwich Shoppe." Victoria felt weirdly vindictive.

"Shame. Sal makes a hell of a club sandwich. You're the boss, though. How do you feel about fried fish?"

"Um. Generally pro, I guess?"

"Cool. Salty's it is."

They drove down Main Street for five blocks. Then Bianca whipped into a sharp left, narrowly dodging an oncoming truck, then into a right down a street so narrow it might have been an alley. Victoria clung to her seat, eyes wide, until Bianca screeched to a stop in front of a small shop with a dirty yellow awning. The battered tin sign above it read *Salty's Fish and Chips*.

The curb she'd parked on was clearly marked as a fire lane. Victoria pointed that out, but Bianca waved her off.

"Won't be here long enough to matter."

"At the restaurant or in town?"

"Either. I doubt I'll be here long after the will reading. Easiest way to avoid tickets is to skip town."

"I don't think it works that way, Ms. Burke."

"Bianca. And yes, it does."

The restaurant didn't have a front door or outdoor seating, just a narrow, nicotine-stained window. Bianca knocked twice on the glass. The cook, an unshaven man of indeterminate age with a paper hat half-covering his sparse hair, slid it open. A half-burned cigarette hung from his wide, almost frog-like mouth.

Bianca held up her fingers. "Two, Wendell, and a couple of Moxies."

The cook grunted and slammed the window shut. Minutes later, he opened it to pass through a pair of red-checked paper trays filled with fries and thick fish fillets, as well as two red cans of cola. Bianca dropped a twenty on the windowsill and handed Victoria hers. It smelled delicious. The two fried fillets were crispy gold, the fries thick and drenched with salt. Victoria didn't even mind being served a Moxie with food this good.

She turned to thank Wendell, but he'd already slammed the window shut.

Bianca nodded in the general direction of south, going up the street. "Come on. Let's see the sights."

"Oh." Victoria followed, trying to juggle her tray and soda while retrieving a fry. "Are we eating and walking?"

"You're sure as hell not eating this greasy crap in *my* car, ladybug." Bianca took an appreciative bite of her fish. "Damn, that's good."

Victoria took a bite of her own. Bianca was right, it was delicious. Probably the exact opposite of healthy and sure to cause heartburn later, but that was Future Vickie's problem. In the moment, it was oh so worth it.

After two blocks of walking, the narrow street opened onto a wide, cobblestoned square. Dozens of people milled about. Some were crossing, on their way from one shop or to another. Others were busily putting up decorations. Orange, red, and yellow bunting stretched from one iron light pole to the next. Four large banners stood at the square's corners, dark red with an eight-armed wheel embroidered in the center with goldenrod thread. Bundles of harvest fruits hung from the banner's pole tops—small gourds, apples and ears of corn. A crow alighted on the crossarm of the closest banner, pecking at the corn.

Wooden scaffolds stood around the edges of the square, each holding a scarecrow. They were lumpy figures of burlap, denim, and flannel, filled with straw. Their overstuffed arms stretched out stiffly, gnarled stick hands reaching for passers-by. Wide stone bowls sat on the ground beneath them, their insides black with scorch marks. Bits of detritus filled the bowls, mostly food waste. As Victoria watched, a young woman leading a small child dropped an apple core into a scarecrow's bowl. The little girl giggled and copied her minder, throwing her half-eaten lollipop after the apple.

A long table stood at the west end of the square. A trio of teenage girls were pulling a large burgundy cloth over it, overseen by a pale woman with long black hair, a dark violet blouse and an impressive amount of eye makeup. When she saw Victoria looking, she gave her a slow wink. Victoria blushed and quickly turned away, bumping into a tall man wearing green flannel and worn overalls.

Victoria was a tall woman, but the severely bearded man loomed over her. His blue eyes were wide beneath bristly black eyebrows, darting back and forth like cerulean fireflies. His mouth twitched beneath his wiry mustache. Victoria took a step back.

"I'm sorry," she stammered.

The big man leaned forward, his shadow falling over her face. Then he reached into the front pocket of his overalls and pulled out a thin stack of white paper. He held it out to her.

"Would you like some lit'racher?" he asked in a surprisingly soft voice.

Without thinking, Victoria took the topmost pamphlet. A wide eye in a circle dominated the front page. Beneath it, the pamphlet asked, "Do You Know What Lies Beyond?" The whole thing looked amateurish but sincere.

"The time is coming," the big man said earnestly. "All will want to hear the truth before it's too late."

This immediately snuffed out the brief spark of reassurance his friendliness had fanned. Fortunately, help was at hand. One moment, Bianca was behind Victoria and to her right. The next, she was standing between Victoria and the strange man, her left palm flat against his chest. She was a full foot shorter than him but looked up as if she were the most intimidating person on the square.

"I'm afraid Ms. Williams isn't in the market for new philosophies." Her voice was firm as tempered steel, as cold as ice. "We'd appreciate if you gave her some *space*."

The tall man blinked once, then took a heavy step backward. He clutched the rest of his pamphlets to his chest like a security blanket. Beneath his bushy beard, he mumbled something that was probably an apology. Another voice broke the tension.

"Jon. You leave those nice folks alone, now."

The second man stood a few yards away. A third large man dressed identically to the first stood beside him. The shorter man wore an open flannel shirt over a thin white undershirt, heavy working boots and a black, wide-brimmed hat. He smiled beneath a stringy brown beard. Jon shuffled over to him, head bowed like a child about to get a scolding.

"My apologies, ladies. My children can get a little enthusiastic about the faith."

Bianca raised one thin eyebrow. It arched imperiously above her sunglass lens. "Keep your flock on a shorter leash, Waylon."

The other big man, a bulky fellow with a bushy red beard and shiny bald pate, glowered at her. Waylon just laughed. He tipped the brim of his hat to Victoria.

"You have a good afternoon, Miz Williams. Perhaps I'll see you after the reading."

Victoria's blood chilled. Bianca placed a firm hand on her shoulder and led her away. Victoria couldn't resist throwing a look back at the proselytizers. Waylon wasn't looking at her anymore, just rocking back on his heels and laughing. Jon snuck a sheepish look at her, giving her a small wave. She returned it with an uncertain smile.

"Stay clear of the Yonders," Bianca said. "They aren't as harmless as everyone thinks."

Victoria glanced at the pamphlet, reading the question again. "The Yonders?"

"They've got a compound a couple miles outside of town. They're a cult, Victoria."

Bianca snatched the pamphlet out of Victoria's hand, balled it up and tossed it into the nearest scarecrow's offering bowl.

"No one's accused them of any actual crimes—*yet*—but that's not surprising for this town."

"What do you mean?"

"I mean that there's an awful lot that goes on under the surface. No one talks about it, especially not to outsiders, but everyone knows. It's just easier to pretend they don't." Bianca shook her head, disgusted. "Makes this gig a hell of a lot harder than it needs to be."

Victoria pondered this quietly for a moment. Then she asked the question that had been lurking at the back of her throat since she met the strange woman.

"Bianca, why are you doing this?"

Bianca looked at her over her round sunglasses. "It's my job, ladybug. My last task from Miz Bruttenholm. 'Keep Victoria safe'. That's what I aim to do."

"But… why?"

The private detective shrugged. "I'm not paid to ask 'why', ladybug. Not of my clients, anyway. Sometimes *they* wanna know why. To be honest, it's usually pretty banal. You'd be amazed what some folks would do for a little bit of money."

Victoria looked away, disappointed. She supposed it was too much to expect this impossibly cool person to be into her, of all people. Instead she looked at the scarecrow hanging from the nearest scaffold.

Bianca didn't seem to notice. That figured. "Now, a *lot* of money, that makes sense. Even just a million. I can understand doing some stupid shit for a million or two. I'm talking *thousands*. Low thousands, at that."

"You don't say."

Victoria's moping was cut short when she got a close look at the scarecrow. The folds in its burlap sack head formed a grimacing face, as if it was angry or in pain.

"This one guy, he faked his own death to get out of three hundred a month in child support. Can you believe that? You know how much a new ID costs? He'd have saved money just mailing his ex a check, *and* his kid would have been taken care of."

From the way the scarecrow's neck bent, it almost looked as if it had been hanged.

"Of course, he's in jail now. Assault charge, after I tracked him down." Bianca chuckled, shaking her head in reminiscence. "He did not want to be found."

*At least they broke its neck*, Victoria thought. *Better than stretching.*

"Most of my cases aren't that exciting," Bianca added quickly. "This one won't be. Just have to babysit you until tonight, then we're both free and clear."

"Plus you get paid." Victoria was unable to keep the sourness out of her voice.

"That's right." Bianca didn't try to hide her annoyance. "I'm protecting you so I get paid. That's the sort of honesty you're not going to get much of in this town, ladybug. Don't turn your nose up at it."

Victoria popped another fry in her mouth as she tried to come up with a response. Bianca's face was inscrutable. She gave Victoria a tight smile, then turned her attention back to the crowd. Victoria followed suit, looking not at the people but the scarecrows hanging from the poles.

What did Wilhelmina Bruttenholm think she'd need protection from?

The closest scarecrow's burlap face offered no answers.

"Come on, ladybug," Bianca called over her shoulder. "Let's see the rest of the town."

## 05

The clouds above Mooncroft Manor were thick and dark. The air tingled, as if a storm was building. Not a tiny shower or a mere bluster, but a real barnstormer, the wrath of the sea blowing over the hills, drenching the countryside as lightning blazed across the sky. A night for Great Works was brewing. It might not be tonight, but it would be coming soon. Nicodemus prayed to the Lords Below that he would have time to prepare.

Judging by the decayed state of the Ruthven's ancestral home, he would need all the help he could get.

The Ruthvens had abandoned Mooncroft Manor a mere three years after he had been cast out, claiming it was too expensive to keep up but unwilling, or perhaps just too wise, to part with the property entirely. It stood empty these seven years, slowly rotting in the seaside air. The roof was in a dreadful state, the wooden siding beginning to fall off the walls, and half the windows were broken. No doubt the work of teenage vandals, out to prove their bravery to one another. At least they'd done no more than that—the house's ill reputation prevented the scoundrels from tagging it and hopefully from breaking in as well.

Hell alone knew how the place looked inside. Nicodemus supposed he ought to find out. It was the only place he would be welcome to stay, and the most likely place to find the answers he sought.

The wrought-iron gates were locked up tight, a length of chain wrapped around them and secured with a heavy padlock. Nicodemus had more than enough art to handle that. A bare two minutes and the lock came undone in his hand, the chain slithering to the ground like a headless steel serpent. The rusty gates protested when he pushed them open, but the land welcomed him as he stepped onto the lot. He picked his way through the overgrown lawn, hopping easily from paver to paver until he reached the porch. He was unsurprised to find the front door locked. The wood groaned beneath his feet, as if the house objected to his strange presence.

"Shhhh…" He stroked the door frame gently, as if reassuring a skittish horse. "I was born in this house. You know me."

The wood trembled beneath his touch. Deep within the house, joists creaked and moaned. He imagined the porch's roof coming lower as the house bent toward him. The doorknob turned easily under his hand, and the house opened to him.

Nicodemus stood in the open door, glancing back over his shoulder. The yard was quiet, save for the rustling of grass and tree branches in the breeze. No living creature stirred. He grinned, fox-sly.

"You can come out now. I know you're there."

Nothing answered him for a long minute. Then Belinda stepped out from behind the big tree. She'd exchanged her silk pajamas for a green blouse and black trousers, and a long wool coat. She bowed her head slightly, a sullen expression on her narrow face.

"How did you know I was there?" she asked.

"You're not as quiet as you think. How did you get here so quickly?"

"You're not as clever as you think."

"Is that so? Pity." He turned back to the open door. "Well, come along, Belle. Let's visit the old homestead."

Belinda struggled through the brush to the porch, the house creaking in protest as soon as she set foot on the steps. "How did you get the door open? Aunt Dolores has the only key."

Nicodemus shrugged. "Haven't a clue. I'm not that clever, remember?"

Belinda stuck her tongue out at him. He laughed and went inside. She hesitated at the threshold, staring into the dark great hall.

A short foyer separated it from the front door, but the inner doors had fallen off their hinges, revealing the cavernous space. The ceiling vaulted to the second floor. Two staircases wrapped around the walls and met in the middle, framing a large portrait. An ornate six-armed chandelier had once hung from the high ceiling; now it lie in ruins in the middle of the room.

"Home again, home again." Nicodemus' malicious good humor was unmistakable. "Jiggity jig."

Belinda shuddered. "This isn't *my* home."

Nicodemus scowled, although not at her. "It's all of our home, Belle. Our *true* home. The restoration of our family fortunes waits within her."

He turned again, holding out his hand. His eyes were gentle, but his expression brooked no refusal. *"Come."*

Belinda hesitated for a moment longer. Aunt Dolores had forbidden them from this place. The twins, who were pills but were also older and theoretically wiser, had warned her against playing in the ruin, against disobeying their great-aunt. Yet, here was Cousin Nickie, back from beyond, beckoning her to do what was forbidden. She took his hand. Clinging to it like a lifeline, she crossed the threshold into Mooncroft Manor.

It occurred to Nicodemus that he probably could have warned her about what would happen next. He'd seen it happen many times before. There was a reason the Ruthven children never brought home playmates, beyond a sense of superiority. Every fine home had its watchdog.

An electric sensation washed over her, as if something burned its way along her nerves. It started at her fingertips, ran up her limbs and across her chest, shot down her spine to her legs, and finally spread through her brain. For a heartbeat, for a lifetime, she knew she was being *watched*. In an eyeblink, the great hall vanished. She stood alone in the center of a wasteland, staring up at a blazing winged figure of emerald fire, bound to the sky in heavy chains. Noxious green clouds swirled around it. The being's light gave off no heat; instead, Belinda's skin felt as if she'd been doused with acid. She threw a hand over her face, but it offered no protection from the emerald glare. Her hand spasmed in agony as skin and flesh dissolved, flaking away to reveal scoured bone. She screamed, falling into Nicodemus' arms.

"There, there, dear cousin." He gently stroked her hair. "You've been seen. You've been welcomed."

Belinda stared at her hand. It was whole, unmarred, the bones hidden beneath the flesh as they should be. She flexed her fingers and looked up at Nicodemus, tears streaming down her face.

"That was *welcoming*?"

"You're still breathing, aren't you? Skin all where it should be? Tears running down your face instead of blood?" Nicodemus placed both hands beneath her arms and raised her up. "You're not eating at the children's table, Belle. The stakes are much higher. Did you think the family manor had been left undefended?"

Taking her by the arm, Nicodemus led Belinda to the portrait on the wall. "The old wizard knew better than that."

The portrait depicted a man in early 19th century garb. His dark coat, padded shoulders, and cinched waist flattered his slight frame, and the high collar did not hide his delicate features. He wore a silver ring with ornate scrollwork on his left hand. In his right, he carried a short copper sword, the astrological symbol for Venus worked into the pommel. He stood beneath a dark, cloudy sky, as ominous as that outside the walls. Two figures appeared in the clouds, each looming over one shoulder. On his left, a tall creature with distinct horns lurked. In the figure on his right, a bolt of lightning had been worked to suggest fangs.

The man was easily recognizable as a Ruthven from his blond hair, narrow chin, and high cheekbones, even without regard to the shield embroidered over his left breast. It was the same shield hanging on the wall above the portrait—the Ruthven shield. Not the old symbol of Clan Ruthven back in the Lowlands; this was the symbol the true Ruthvens had adopted when they abandoned Scotland for the Continent rather than give up the family name. It was a green field—*vert*—upon which was charged a black serpent biting its own tail. The Ruthvens claimed publicly it was to represent the family's endurance and restoration, although Nicodemus knew better. The serpent tied in with the shield's topper—a goat's horns and a pair of bat's wings, worked in black metal. Beneath the shield, a silver scroll sported their motto: *Venia Virtutes Aeta Bibimus*.

"Graham Ruthven," Nicodemus said approvingly. "Our forefather."

"I've never heard of him," Belinda said.

Nicodemus *tsked*. "A shame, but not your own."

He pointed to the signature in the portrait's bottom right corner. She read it aloud. "Vernon Pickman, '55. Pickman?"

Nicodemus nodded. "Your great-grandfather, on your father's side. Quite a clever man, from what I've gathered. Auntie Dearest must have been trying to capture some of that cleverness when she arranged for your parents' marriage. Didn't stop her from letting them raise you as a Pickman."

"I don't understand."

"I'm trying to explain." He gestured to the portrait again. "Here's where it all begins. Old Graham brought us to America after some… controversy in Germany."

"What sort of controversy?"

"One involving heresy and secret societies, no doubt." Nicodemus bared sharp teeth in an approving smile. "Grandfather Graham was a very eccentric man. He came to these shores with his elder sister and younger brother a little under two centuries ago. He built this whole house… and mastered its guardian."

A draft blew through the great hall, cool and stale. After a moment, a second followed it. Then a third, as if the old house was breathing.

"Come along, Belle. There's still more to see."

He led her not up the stairs but through the doorway on the east side. A long hallway wound around the great hall and through the building. Belinda flicked the light switch to no result; the family clearly hadn't been paying the power bill. Nicodemus made an irritated noise when she turned on the light in her phone.

"What?" Belinda said, annoyed. "I can't see in the dark."

He blinked his emerald eyes. "You can't?"

"Of course not!"

"We'll have to do something about that. Very well, carry on. Don't aim it at my face."

The long-abandoned hall lacked dust, but the ceilings were choked with cobwebs. The dark wallpaper was peeling in places, and wet stains on the ceiling and hardwood floors told of leaks. More portraits hung from the walls, depicting Ruthvens of the past. Some bore Vernon Pickman's signature, others that of later Pickmans, some few of unknown artists. Several paintings had been ruined by mice and mildew. Others were torn, as if slashed by knives. A rare few were unmarred. Those Ruthvens stared at the cousins as they passed.

"I can't tell if they approve of us or not." Belinda's voice echoed down the hall.

"Almost certainly not, for reasons both foul and fair," Nicodemus said cheerfully. "We're not traditionally the most loving family."

Nicodemus stopped at a stairwell in the back of the house. It led down, not up. When Belinda commented her surprise, he flashed her a grim smile.

"Some gently bred families hide their shame in the attic. We Ruthvens prefer to lock ours away beneath the earth."

"What—" she began, stopping when Nicodemus jerked his head up like a hound catching a scent. He grabbed her and pulled her into a side room, clapping his hand over her mouth to stifle her protest. He hissed in her ear to shut off her ridiculous light. She thumbed it off without thinking.

Another shaft of light cut through the gloom. Heavy footsteps clomped down the hall, followed by a thin voice.

"I don't know what you kids are doing here, but you'd better skedaddle. This is private property, you hear?"

Nicodemus let Belinda go and carefully pushed her away, gesturing for her to remain silent. He crouched behind the door, listening to the stranger stomp down the hall. As soon as the other man had passed, Nicodemus dove through the doorway and grabbed him, holding a long knife to the other's stubbly throat.

"Oh, it's private property, all right," Nicodemus said, entirely too cheerfully. "*My* private property."

"You let me go now!" the other man gasped. "I'll summon the sheriff! Don't think I won't!"

Belinda recognized the reedy voice. She poked her head out of the doorway and rolled her eyes. "Oh, Nickie, let him go. It's just Waits."

Claude Waits, the hereditary groundskeeper, turned his head around as carefully as he could with the very sharp knife pressed to his throat. Not carefully enough; the blade nicked his rough skin. The stream of blood distracted Nicodemus, but he recognized the old man now.

"Claude! You're alive!" He let Waits go, giving him a mostly friendly shove. "First Monty and now you. It's true what they say, only the good die young."

"Very droll, Master Nicodemus." Waits fished a dirty handkerchief from his back pocket, dabbing it to his throat. "Last I heard you weren't to return."

"I heard that too." Nicodemus returned the knife to its sheath inside his coat. "Yet here I am. You're falling down on the job,

Claude. The house looks like shit."

Waits wrung his tweed flat cap between his hands, cringing. "I'm very sorry, Master Nicodemus. Things aren't as they were. I do what I can, but there's no money for upkeep no more. Your family all moved out. Don't even have the lights on no more."

"I don't care about the electricity." Nicodemus sniffed, looking around the musty hallway. "I can do without it. Water's a different matter. I'm accustomed to flush toilets."

"Master Nicodemus?"

"There's a Ruthven in residence again." Nicodemus clapped him on the shoulder. "Get the water running. By tomorrow, if it's no trouble. Then start cleaning this dump up."

"Master Nicodemus? I don't…"

"I said *get the water running*, Claude. I don't care *how* you do it, just *do it*. What else are you good for? It certainly isn't mowing the lawn."

"Of… of course, sir! Right away, sir!"

The old man scurried off, his muttering echoing incoherently down the hall. Nicodemus shook his head.

"Ridiculous old man. The family needs a better class of servants."

"I've always thought so," Belinda said. "I have some ideas."

"I'm sure you do, pet. We'll have plenty of time to put them into action. In the meantime, there's something I want you to see."

He led her down the stairs into the basement. It was unfinished, damp and cold. A heavy steel door stood in the wall.

Someone had drawn an odd symbol on its surface, a downward-pointing star in a circle, surrounded by geomantic figures—not a pentagram, but something more complex. Above it hung the Ruthven crest. The door had been locked, once, and covered in thick chains. Now it hung open, the chains strewn across the floor in messy coils. There was no point in locking it now.

Nicodemus stood at the doorway, one hand on the door, and stared inside. It was a single cavernous room, strewn with debris, stained with blood, tinged with sorrow. He couldn't bring himself to go in, to disturb its funereal silence. Despite everything he was, the memories of this place nearly brought him to tears.

"I know about this," Belinda said, her voice a silver chirp in the dark. "Lavinia told me. The family used to keep a monster down here."

"A monster!" Nicodemus whirled around, rage burning in his eyes. "He was no monster! He was my brother! Your cousin, Enoch!"

Belinda stumbled backward, cringing more from Nicodemus' sudden rage than at this revelation. "What?"

Nicodemus scowled, his face a sinister mask. "Enoch Ruthven. My older brother. Dolores was afraid of him, when he got too big, so she had him locked away down here. Mother tried to stop her. Dolores doesn't take opposition well, especially not from within the family."

"Your father let her do that?"

"My father wasn't Enoch's father."

He shuddered at the memory. He'd still been small. The hired men had dragged his mother away, Meredith Ruthven spitting curses all the way. His father held him by the shoulder, holding him back. It was the only moment of strength Ezekiel Ruthven had ever shown.

They'd taken her out into the woods, to the secret shed Dolores kept there. He'd never seen her again.

He remembered when the basement was… not homey, but lively. He'd occasionally wheedled his way into helping at feeding time. He remembered his brother's asymmetrical bulk in the shadows, the strength and warmth of his arms, his honeyed voice. Enoch sang to him sometimes, songs of the things that danced between the stars and crawled beneath the earth, songs of blood and stone and nightmare. He had been beautiful and terrible. By the powers, Nicodemus missed him so.

He drew himself back up, forcing the rage back into his stomach where it belonged, where heat and pressure would turn raw fury into a diamond of revenge. His face was calm but stern, his green eyes bright.


Nicodemus was a short, slight man, yet he filled Belinda's view. Her beloved cousin, her favorite cousin. In her childish memory, he was a dark prince who'd cared for her when everyone else thought she was a nuisance. Now, as practically an adult, he was just a man… yet somehow more. Energy rose from him like summer heat. She couldn't take her eyes off him.

"You wanted to know why they chased me out of town?" His

voice was mild yet brimming with long-simmering hatred. "It was because I let Enoch out. I let him out, and it caused trouble, and the people of this rotten town killed him. So I killed one of them back."

Nicodemus turned to the seal on the door, sneering. "And do you know what the family did then?"

Belinda nodded solemnly, understanding blossoming within her young mind. "They turned on you."

"Exactly. I had defied Auntie Dearest. Defied her and upset her plans."

He brushed his fingers over the Ruthven crest's scrollwork. "'We Drink Deeply The Vein Of Power'. That's no idle boast. The world is full of powers. Old Wizard Graham found one. Auntie Dearest thinks she's found another. She's wrong, and that's why the family has fallen so."

Nicodemus held out his hand to her, eyes blazing emerald in the dark. Belinda felt her nerves burn again, electricity running down her spine and through her limbs. She felt as if she stood on the edge of a great precipice, a vast void above her, an endless abyss yawning beneath.

"Join me, Belle. Help me restore the Ruthvens to their rightful place."

Belinda stared into his luminous eyes. Her hand lifted of its own accord. The things he was saying, the things he'd shown her, they were absurd. Yet, she knew Aunt Dolores had been hiding things from her. She knew she was, at best, a backup in whatever schemes her aunt was spinning. Meanwhile, here was

Nicodemus, her beloved Nickie, back after a decade's absence, and *he* wanted *her.*

She took his hand. He wrapped his bony fingers around hers and smiled, foxlike. A warm shudder shook her slight form.

*"Very good,"* he said.

"What do we do now?"

"First, we need to find out what Wilhelmina Bruttenholm knew. I want to know the state of the board before I make a move."

Belinda pouted. "Aunt Dolores said I couldn't go to the will reading."

Nicodemus inclined his head and offered her his arm. "And Cousin Nickie says you shall."

## 06

It was getting dark when Bianca drove Victoria back to Huntingdon Abbey, although it was hard to tell if that was due to the lateness of the hour or the ominous clouds building in the sky.

"Gonna be a bastard of a storm," Bianca said cheerily, forced to remove her shades.

"A good night to be inside," Victoria said.

Despite the chill and the threatening storm, Mercy remained outside, working. She was putting up scarecrows around the parking lot. Six scaffolds ringed the gravel square. She'd already hung three of the effigies and was struggling with a fourth when Bianca's car pulled in. The scarecrows were much like those in the town square, overstuffed figured dressed as farmers, but these had genuine faces embroidered on their burlap heads. Not pleasant ones, mind—they were scowling or screaming, like men waiting for the gallows.

Victoria thought they were creepy but fun. She was starting to like this town. She called out to Mercy, "They look really cool!"

Mercy threw a withering look over her shoulder. "Oh, are our rustic traditions quaint enough for you, townie?"

Victoria flinched, but Bianca put a reassuring hand on her shoulder. "Ignore her, ladybug. She's an awkward bitch, but basically harmless."

Mercy gave Bianca the finger. Bianca laughed, unbothered, and gently guided Victoria toward the steps leading her up the hill. Victoria let herself be pushed, stung by Mercy's rudeness.

"I don't understand why she reacted that way," Victoria said, her voice low so that only Bianca could hear her. "I was being genuine."

"Because people like that can't handle genuine emotion," Bianca said, a touch more loudly than conversational voice. "She's just miserable, and she doesn't know how not to be miserable, so she lashes out at the people around her. Like a hurt animal that doesn't know any better."

Victoria glanced over her shoulder. Mercy was still trying to hang the fourth scarecrow from its scaffold, but now she was glaring daggers at the two of them. Victoria ducked her head, momentarily ashamed for flinching, and focused her attention on the steps ahead of her.

Once at the door, Bianca slipped smoothly around Victoria and opened it for her. "Now, me, I found something I love doing and threw myself into it, and behold! A confident, pleasant woman stands before you."

"Something you love doing?" Victoria said, unable to keep the unmistakable note of interest out of her voice.

"Traveling around the country and getting into trouble." She winked at Victoria. "Maybe I'll tell you some stories after the reading."

Victoria blushed. "I'd like that."

Bianca grinned back. "Good."

They walked through the lobby together. Victoria wasn't sorry to see Bianca still following her, but it felt a bit awkward now. She wasn't sure what the private eye was thinking. Mercy had said there were rules against visitors in the rooms, hadn't she?

"Um. I think I can make it to my room on my own." Victoria wrung the hem of her shirt between her hands, looking down at her feet.

"I'm sure you can, ladybug." Bianca smirked. "I'm staying here too."

Victoria flushed beet red. "Oh!"

"Yeah. Now that you're back safe and sound, I can get on with the rest of my work. I have a few things to do in order to get ready for the reading. Unless there's something else you need first?"

Victoria laughed awkwardly. There were a couple of things that came to mind, but she wanted Bianca to take her out on an actual date first. "I'm so sorry, I didn't mean to keep you from your job."

"This *is* my job, ladybug." Bianca tapped Victoria lightly

on the nose. "I have to say, this afternoon was one of my more pleasurable assignments."

"I had a fun time, too," Victoria said quickly. "Thank you for watching out for me."

"Thank *you* for mostly staying out of trouble. I've had details who didn't want to listen. Makes the job a hundred times harder. I'd watch your back anytime."

Victoria found herself grinning like a fool. She hid her face behind her hair in a vain attempt to recover some of her dignity. Then she brushed it away, feeling suddenly bold. "Well, if you need to reach me, I'm in room 303."

"I know. I'm in 206. Just in case."

"Should I give you my phone number?"

Bianca pulled out her phone and tapped the screen a couple of times. Victoria's phone buzzed. An unknown caller had sent her a winky face emoji.

"Oh."

"I've had your contact info for a while, actually. Part of the job." Bianca winked. "Don't worry. I promise not to sell your information for anything less than a lot of money."

"When you're already getting paid for this job."

"That's right. Only reason I'm watching you."

"I'll bet." Victoria smiled, more confidently this time. "I'll see you in a bit, Ms. Burke."

"Later, ladybug."

Victoria knew Bianca watched her go up to the third-floor landing, but when she looked over her shoulder, Bianca had disappeared into the second-floor hallway. Victoria was a little sad to see her go; she hadn't expected to like her so much. She hadn't expected to like the town so much, for that matter. Sure, she'd only seen a little bit of it, but it had a unique atmosphere, and most of the people seemed friendly enough. Except for Mercy. And Nicodemus.

Well, that wasn't true. Nicodemus had certainly been friendly, in a weird, off-putting sort of way, or at least had tried to be. She still couldn't shake the feeling that there was something untrustworthy about him. Maybe it was just his attitude.

Once back in her room, Victoria looked around again. It didn't take long. The space was sparse, but she supposed she didn't need much. Not for the one night. The bed looked less than inviting and only big enough for one, and looking at the bedsheets and pillow, she now keenly wished she'd thought to bring her own. Still, it was adequate. She gave the bed a test sit, plopping herself down in the middle. The metal frame squeaked noisily, but it held. She expected to fall in, but it didn't sag at all.

It occurred to her that most likely, not many people had slept here.

Victoria leaned back on the bed, hands behind her head, and wondered what she was supposed to do for the next couple of hours. She only brought the one book, which she'd finished on the train. She hadn't brought her sketchbook; she hadn't even brought her Nintendo Switch. It hadn't occurred to her that she might be bored. She hadn't put a lot of thought into this trip, if she was being honest with herself. Maybe Tina was right, maybe she was being inappropriately impulsive. Maybe she ought to text her roommate and let her know she'd arrived safe, like she promised she would.

Before she could open her text app, a scuttling sound at the end of the room reminded her of her latest roommate. She got up and checked the box on the dresser. The tarantula looked up at her with eight unblinking eyes, huddled in the corner. She was such a striking figure. Now that Victoria had the time to admire her, the white smudge on her abdomen looked weirdly like a skull. It went well with the white stripes running down her legs, which resembled bones. She waved her two front legs at Victoria. Something about the movement seemed sluggish. Victoria remembered what Tabitha had said about the climate not being good for tarantulas. It was rather chilly in here—Huntingdon Abbey's remodeling evidently hadn't included insulation or ventilation. A radiator sat in the opposite corner, hissing and clicking merrily away, but it was only heating that quarter of the room. Poor Samantha—Victoria had decided the tarantula looked like a Samantha—wasn't getting much benefit from it. Victoria was hardly getting any benefit herself.

Well, Samantha certainly hadn't asked to come up here. Victoria was going to have to make sure she got settled somewhere and not casually discarded. She figured her best bet in the short term was to ask for help downstairs. Mercy might be a bitch, but she looked like the sort of person who knew about spiders.

"Don't worry, Samantha." Victoria picked up the shoebox,

cradling it carefully. "Just a quick trip downstairs."

She'd expected to find Mercy in the lobby behind the front desk, or failing that, still in the parking lot struggling with scarecrows. Instead, both areas were empty, although it looked like the scarecrows had all been put up. Victoria wasn't exactly sorry to have missed Mercy. At the same time, she needed to talk to *someone* about her new friend. She certainly wasn't going to take Samantha out in the cold to go looking for Mercy—it was even colder outside!

Victoria went back up the hall, resigning herself to moving the dresser closer to the radiator, when she heard a voice coming from the second door on the left, with a sign that said *Kitchen*. It sounded like someone singing. Probably not Mercy, but maybe someone who could help. Victoria carefully shouldered the door open and saw the coolest person she'd ever met in front of the sink.

They were tall, with light brown skin and tightly coiled hair dyed purple, shaved close on the sides but long on top. They wore a long, black sleeveless coat and striped tights, as well as knee-high high-heeled boots that were utterly impractical for the kitchen but necessary for the aesthetic. Colorful tattoos ran up their bare arms, and their complicated eye makeup was immaculate. Their food-stained white apron was hilariously incongruous but detracted nothing from their overall look. Neither did the annoyed glance they flashed Victoria when they heard the door open.

"Kitchen's off-limits to guests, honey."

"I'm sorry!" Victoria pushed her way through the door anyway, holding the shoebox out in front of her. "I'm just looking for some advice for, well, a new friend."

It occurred to her a second too late that it might not be the best of ideas to bring what was technically vermin into the kitchen. Fortunately, the cook's expression when they lifted the lid was one of delight.

"What a big girl!" they said, eyes bright.

"Her name is Samantha," Victoria said proudly.

They nodded. "She looks like a Samantha."

They put their hand into the box. Samantha skittered up their arm, resting on their forearm over a green tattoo of the Bride of Frankenstein. The cook cooed at her.

"Where did she come from? Maine isn't the climate for critters like this, especially not in the fall."

"Well …" Victoria made a face, knowing how this story was going to sound. "She sort of appeared in the pocket of my ride from the station. Tabitha. You know Tabitha Swann?"

The cook made a face. It might have been a grin. It might have been a grimace. "I know Tabitha."

Inwardly, Victoria kicked herself. Of course they knew Tabitha. Everyone probably knew everyone here. She was the stranger.

Well, she was going to fix that. "I'm Victoria Williams."

The corner of the cook's mouth turned up, a clear smirk. "I know."

Victoria flustered. "You know?"

"You're the only face in the Abbey I don't recognize. That must belong to the only name I'm not familiar with." They offered their hand. "Thorn Hale."

Victoria felt an electric touch when their hands touched. Oh, hell. Was this going to happen *every* time she met a new femme in this town?

She imagined Tina smirking behind her, saying, *If your past history is anything to go by? Yes.*

Victoria flashed a quick smile, hoping to banish her nerves. "I don't suppose you know anything about this cute little creature?"

"Quite a bit, actually." Thorn smiled down at the spider. "First, I know a cardboard box is no place for 'em."

"I figured that." Victoria flushed. "This was just a temporary solution. So she didn't get hurt in the truck."

"Good thinking." Thorn let Samantha skitter back into the box. "They like it warm. Warmer than we can get it upstairs this time of year, I'm afraid. You'll want to get her an aquarium, ideally with a heating pad. There's a pet store on Main. It'll be closed now, though."

"Maybe I can pick one up in the morning before I catch the train," said Victoria, who definitely couldn't afford that.

Thorn nodded, pleased. "Good idea. You can also get crickets for her to eat. She should only need a couple a week. She looks pretty full now, though. Don't you, baby?"

Victoria couldn't help but feel warm at the endearing way Thorn cooed at Samantha. They were definitely a spider person. She'd never met a spider person before.

"So, if it's not a good idea to keep her in my room…"

"She can stay down here. It's plenty warm, and it'll stay that way even when we shut the oven off for the night."

"You're sure? Won't someone say something?

Thorn's grin widened. "Not to me. I only answer to Her, and she pretty much gives me the run of the place."

"Thank you!" Victoria set the box down on the kitchen counter, far from the sink. "I promise I'll be back for her."

"I know you will," Thorn winked. "And if you're not, I know where you're staying."

Victoria laughed as she went back out the door, blushing.

Bianca's room didn't come with a closet—the three to four nuns who once slept there probably didn't need one, only having an outfit apiece—so a small tower of file boxes stood in one corner. They held the fruits of a life's work—decades of research, to which Bianca was proud to have added a small piece.

Tabitha Swann and her friends would kill for them—so would half the great and good of Ravenkirk. This was Wilhelmina Bruttenholm's personal archive, records on every person of prominence in Ravenkirk and a few outside it, organized in concise dossiers. As one of Bruttenholm's final instructions, they were to be passed on to specific people during her will reading. It was an unusual request, but Bianca had dealt with odder jobs. The check waiting for her when the assignment was complete would make it all worthwhile.

Not that she minded being paid to hang out with a cutie like Victoria Williams. Wouldn't Ladybug be surprised when she read her file? It was hard, sometimes, being under a gag order, but Bruttenholm had paid for discretion as well as competence. Victoria would probably understand, and if she didn't? There would be other jobs, other towns, and other gals.

Bianca double-checked the time. The will reading would be in a couple of hours; time to get this show on the road. The women who worked at the Abbey were supposed to set up the common room for the reading, but the executor had insisted Bianca maintain control of Bruttenholm's files until he arrived. Gray wasn't due to arrive for another hour, but she hated leaving things to the last minute. Time to haul the records down to the drawing room.

She stacked the boxes onto her little collapsible dolly and rolled them down the hall and to the stairs. It would have been nice to hope that Gray would be waiting for her—that way she wouldn't have to spend the next hour guarding the boxes but in a more comfortable room—but the phlegmatic lawyer had been a stickler for his schedule. Neither early nor late, like a wizard but much less exciting.

Still, it was good to see that Harper's girls had done their job. The drawing room was all set up for the reading. The furniture had been pushed to the walls, with thirty wooden chairs set up in clusters of five because God knew these people couldn't be trusted to mix civilly. Bianca had only spent a few months in Ravenkirk, broken up over two years, but she'd uncovered enough to know the power dynamic was tense. If there wasn't blood spilled tonight, it would be a miracle.

The chairs were grouped in a wide arc facing an ornate table. Someone had set up a portrait of the deceased. Wilhelmina Bruttenholm was short but far from slight, wearing a charcoal gray and burgundy suit that did not hide her athletic build … at least, in her youth, when Vernon Pickman painted it. She sat in an ornate chair, an enigmatic smile on her face. Pickman had captured her so well that Bianca could almost see the mischievous twinkle in her eye. She was certainly going to cause trouble tonight, even from beyond the grave. Bianca imagined she was proud of that, wherever she was.

Well, there was no sense wasting time. Bianca unloaded the file boxes, lining them up on the table where Gray could easily access them. She suspected he'd creak if he had to bend over.

No sooner had she thought that than she heard a creak behind her, like a rusty hinge swinging. She jumped bolt upright, one hand going for the pistol beneath her leather jacket. The noise sounded like it came from the wall on her right. There wasn't supposed to be a door on that wall, just a wooden triptych depicting a woman in three stages of her life, standing beneath moon phases. The left panel hung ajar, revealing a dark space in the wall.

Bianca drew her pistol. She couldn't help but grin at the sight. A secret passage. There was an honest-to-God secret passage in the Abbey. What a weird fucking town this was.

She slid across the room, moving silently so as not to trip her intruder. She crept up to the hanging panel, holding her breath as she placed her free hand on the edge. In one fluid motion, she threw the door open and lunged behind it with a shout, aiming her pistol at the intruder.

Only there was no intruder. There *was* a secret passage, a narrow crawlspace within the walls. It was just wide enough for one person to creep silently along, if they didn't breathe too deeply, but no one was inside it. There was only one direction they could have gone. The passage ran three yards to the exterior wall, where it ended with a ladder going down into the cellar. Bianca wanted to follow it, but she didn't dare. She couldn't leave these files alone.

Instead, she closed the secret door slowly and moved a wide loveseat in front of it. She piled it with heavy objects scoured from around the room, then covered the whole thing with a cloth. Hopefully that would deter whoever was sneaking around. She could investigate the secret passage after the will reading. She wondered how extensive it was, and if there were any more.

A chill ran up her spine. It suddenly occurred to her that she should check on Victoria.

Bianca holstered her pistol and fumbled for her phone. She was just about to call Victoria when strong arms grabbed her from behind. One hand clamped around her forehead. Before she could shout or act, a sharp pain slashed across her throat.

Then everything went red, but not for very long.

Victoria went downstairs at half-past seven. She thought she was early—hopefully early enough to get a good seat in the common room. From the number of people waiting in the lobby and hallway, she was clearly mistaken.

In fairness to her, she hadn't realized how hard it was going to be to put her one fancy dress on without Tina's help. The ruffled skirt and sleeves were flowing, but the bodice was rather tight, since it was not cut with her broad ribcage in mind. She supposed she ought to have bought a size higher and gotten the rest taken in, but who could afford that? She could barely afford the dress in the first place.

She'd worried the dress, a black outer dress with a dark violet chemise she'd gotten from an online store specializing in Ren Faire attire, would stand out too much, not that it had stopped her. She realized at once she couldn't look too outrageous for this crowd. For an allegedly sleepy seaside town, the people of Ravenkirk favored outré attire. At least, those who'd been invited to Ms. Bruttenholm's will reading.

There was the clump of women she already knew, hanging out at the front desk and dressed as if they were going to hit the local Goth club afterward. Thorn, Mercy, the black-haired woman from the town square, and a redhead in tall boots. They stood more or less back-to-back, keeping an eye on everyone else.

Tabitha Swann hung back in a corner of the lobby, still wearing her charcoal and burgundy coat. Her arms were folded across her chest as her gaze swung steadily across the guests. Two others joined her, a short Latine woman with messy black hair and a tall man who somehow, in this the Year of Our Lady Gaga 2023, looked like a dandy. All three wore black ribbons around their right arms, a sign of mourning.

A group of Talbots clustered at the opposite end of the lobby. Their elder was a short, stocky woman in a fur-trimmed brown coat; Victoria noted with distaste that it was probably real. Hannah Talbot stood with her, joined by two men of similar age; Victoria guessed that the older woman—Eleanor, she would shortly learn—was probably their grandmother. They had the look of folks who had put on their Sunday best and weren't comfortable in it. The men's hair and beards were too slick with pomade, Hannah's red hair pulled into an uncomfortable bun, incongruous with her shaved sides. Eleanor Talbot let her own wild hair flow free, the privilege of an older woman who'd clearly stopped caring what others thought about her.

The Gilmans hung out in the hallway, the taller of the two men casting furtive glances at the common room door as if he feared someone else might get through it first. There were four of them: a tall man, Gordon Gilman; Abigail, a woman her age; a teenage boy named Cole and their own family's matriarch, Patience Gilman. She was a heavyset woman bent over a sturdy cane. All but the teenager shared wide mouths, broad foreheads, and wide-set eyes. Unlike the others, the Gilmans hadn't made a point of dressing up; the men wore simple flannel shirts and slacks, the women sensible gray dresses. On top of that, Patience wore a sea-green headscarf that covered everything but her wide eyes.

The last knot of people had to have been the Ruthvens. All three had a distinct similarity of features they shared with Nicodemus—high cheekbones, narrow chins, and a haughty air so abrasive it could sand furniture. A tall, severe woman who appeared to be in her sixties stood in the middle of the lobby like a general come to observe a battlefield—their matriarch, Dolores. A man and woman stood with her, both in their early thirties—the twins, Basil and Lavinia. Basil looked like an athlete (not football, but a less popular sport played at elite schools) while Lavinia looked like a butch corporate executive. Basil wore a black suit with a gold tie and pocket square, Lavinia a white suit with a gold blouse. Dolores wore a black shawl over a goldenrod evening gown. She glared dourly at the other families, as if affronted by their presence.

Every eye turned to Victoria as she walked down the hall. An unmistakable aura of hostility sizzled in the air. She tensed, wondering what they were seeing. Had any of them clocked her, or was that just suspicion of outsiders? She nearly froze on the spot. She wanted to turn and flee back to her room, hiding there until morning when she could escape on the train. This had been a mistake from the start. She had no business here, in this town where she didn't know anyone. Best to cut her losses and run.

Then Tabitha took a break from scowling at the Abbey crowd and gave her a wink and a smile. Relief washed through her. She knew at least one person here. Two, if you counted Thorn, who hadn't looked at her yet but had been welcoming earlier. She could get through this.

Victoria walked past the Gilmans, ignoring their glares burning into her back. She passed between the Ruthvens and the Abbey crowd, momentarily burning from the tension between them. The elder Ruthven stared down her long nose at Victoria, as if she was a gatecrasher at a posh party. Well, maybe she was. Victoria resisted the urge to stick her tongue out, instead turning her back to the Ruthvens. They were nothing to do with her, after all.

She paused at the front desk. Mercy glared at her, but the other two women smiled and Thorn raised a silent eyebrow. Victoria tried to look friendly and offered Thorn her hand.

"Thanks again for your help earlier," she said. "How's Samantha?"

"She's doing just fine." Thorn grinned warmly. "I gave her

some water in an old jar lid, and she looked pretty happy. How's your room?"

"You'd better not have made a mess of it," Mercy said, scowl deepening.

Victoria almost flinched. Then she remembered the way Bianca had stood up for her in the town square. She'd been so cool. Maybe Victoria could be that cool. Especially when she'd done nothing to deserve Mercy's scorn.

"I barely have enough stuff to make a mess." Victoria put her hands on her hips. "You saw the suitcase I rolled in. I don't see what I've done to deserve your attitude, and frankly, I don't appreciate it."

"Yeah, fuck you, Chambers," the shorter woman with Tabitha called out.

A chuckle rippled around the room, at least among the younger folks. Their elders looked at the vulgarity with disgust, but Victoria's peers were clearly amused. Even Mercy's friends stifled smirks. Or perhaps they weren't friends at all. Mercy certainly didn't look to them for support, just folded her arms across her chest and fumed.

"Don't worry, Ms. Williams," the dark-haired woman said over Mercy's head. "If you make a mess, we'll send Mercy up to clean it."

"It's her job," the redhead added.

Victoria felt lighter, as if she might float out of her boots. The folks in this town weren't so bad! Tina was wrong; there was nothing to fear here. She was making friends!

"I'll keep that in mind!" she said, voice bright.

Thorn gestured at the other two women. "You've met Mercy, for your sins. The redhead's Alison and Gother-Than-Thou is Tzipporah."

"Pleased to meet you." Victoria looked over her shoulder at the trio in the corner. "Excuse me, I'm going to say 'hi' to Tabitha real quick."

She realized immediately that was the wrong thing to say. The Abbey crew's friendliness immediately melted away, replaced by frozen insincere smiles. Victoria didn't understand what exactly she'd done, but they didn't give her a chance. Thorn turned their back on her, and the others followed suit, closing ranks around the desk. Mercy gave her a quick sneer before turning away, as if she'd won after all.

Victoria took a hesitant step back, looking around as if someone might offer an explanation. None was forthcoming. The elder Ruthven stared at her with unmistakable curiosity, as if she was an animal that might be about to do a clever trick. Lavinia turned up her nose in aloof distaste, while the Talbots in the back stared at her with unmistakable distrust. The Gilmans muttered to themselves but didn't look her way. Tabitha and her friends stared at her expectantly, waiting for her to come to their corner already.

When she finally did, the fancy man smiled, somewhat sadly. "I'm afraid local politics in this sleepy little burg are a bit fraught."

"That's saying something." Tabitha looked apologetic.

"Wilhelmina kind of threw you into it."

"I don't understand," Victoria said.

"Everyone hates everyone else. Mostly the Ruthvens and the Talbots." The short woman tossed her head at the family in the corner. "But they've managed to mix it up with the Gilmans too, lately."

So the trio in the middle *were* Nicodemus' family. Victoria was just about to ask what the trouble was about when Lavinia smiled at them.

"Don't think we've forgotten about your little book club, Tabby dear. Things will be different now that Wilhelmina's not around to protect you."

"Fuck off, Lavinia," the short woman said cheerfully. "You've never scared *me*."

"Megan," the fancy man said.

"Freddie," Megan said back, unbothered.

"*Both* of you." Tabitha put a hand to her head. "Victoria, meet Megan Ruiz and Frederic Drake. We all used to work with Wilhelmina."

Victoria was just about to ask what sort of work that was when the front door flew open. The devil she hadn't spoken of had appeared. Nicodemus Ruthven sauntered through the door, a dour teenage girl in an emerald and black dress in tow. He didn't say a word, only leered nastily at everyone, and the room rose in an uproar. The Gilmans hissed and spat at him, the older man having to physically restrain Abigail, who'd tried to lunge at Nicodemus, teeth bared and fingers like claws. The Abbey crew clustered together, now not in exclusion but for protection. The Talbots likewise clustered around their elder, fists balled and at the ready, while Eleanor eyed Nicodemus as if she was tracking a fox creeping around the henhouse. Only Tabitha and her friends remained calm, and Victoria suspected that was because Tabitha had already run into him.

Nicodemus stood in the doorway, unmistakably basking in the attention. He smiled, eyes flicking snakelike behind his round shades.

"What a warm welcome," he said, clearly relishing the sound of his own voice. "It's good to be home."

The elder Gilman glared at Tabitha and the oldest Ruthven.

"What's he doing here?" she said. Her voice was thick, as if she was gargling saltwater.

"This is no doing of mine, Patience Gilman," Dolores said tiredly.

Nicodemus slid across the floor, bowing theatrically and producing the black envelope. Its gilt edges glittered in the lights. He brandished it like a talisman.

"I ought to just pin this to my coat. Isn't it obvious, Goody Gilman? I was *invited*."

Abigail Gilman's head snapped around to glare at Tabitha's group. She glowered, muttering something in a language Victoria didn't recognize. She wasn't alone. One of the big Talbot men actually bared his teeth and growled at them. Victoria, standing between Tabitha's group and everyone else, suddenly felt as if a spotlight had fallen on her until Tabitha stepped around her, holding her hands up for peace.

"Don't look at us. This is Wilhelmina's last will and testament. Emphasis on *Wilhelmina's*. We're just here to see her last wishes carried out."

"Yeah, you think we'd invite *Nicodemus* of all people if we had the slightest choice?" Megan added.

"Ah, Ms. Ruiz. Glad to see you're as charming as ever," Nicodemus said.

"Bite me."

The elder Ruthven's voice cut through the room. "Enough of everyone's squabbling. Let's get this over with so we can get back to our own lives, and my wayward nephew can return to his exile."

If she'd hoped that would quiet the room, she was sorely mistaken. The noise only grew louder, as the Talbots and Gilmans began shouting at the Ruthvens, then each other. The din was terrifying, but Victoria was grateful that at least everyone had stopped staring at her.

The shouting ended abruptly when a door at the end of the hallway slammed open. Another older woman emerged, wearing a deep blue dress and a sly smirk. She held the arm of a tall, thin man with sallow skin sealed in a tight, unfashionable suit. Victoria recognized them immediately—he was Morris Gray, Esq., the executor of Wilhelmina's estate, and she was the woman in the portrait in the Abbey's lobby, just a couple of decades older. That must make her Maledicta Harper, and by the set of her jaw Mistress Harper was not amused by all the commotion.

"Now, is this any way to behave at a funeral?" She let go of Gray's arm and stomped into the lobby, thumping her cane on the hardwood floor. "Thorn, I thought you knew how to keep the peace around here."

"We do," Tzipporah said, visibly irked. "We avoid putting all of these assholes in one room together."

"Hush, Zip," Thorn said. "Things were going smoothly, Mistress Harper, until the last beneficiary arrived."

They cast their eyes to Nicodemus, who leaned against the wall and smiled beatifically. Maledicta glared up at Gray, looking for confirmation. The gaunt lawyer nodded once and shrugged. She sighed, leaning on her cane.

"I suppose it was too much to expect Wilhelmina to care about what happened after she was gone." Maledicta scowled at Nicodemus. "Can I trust you to keep a civil tongue for one evening, Mister Ruthven?"

"*I* haven't done anything provocative." Nicodemus spread his hands innocently. "I didn't even arrive fashionably late."

"It's true," Thorn said with visible reluctance. "Although he's only been here a few minutes."

"This is outrageous, Maledicta," Patience said. "You cannot expect us to tolerate his presence. He is a vile abomination and an outlaw."

The elder Ruthven bristled. "I'll not permit you to slander my family in my presence, Patience Gilman."

Maledicta thumped her cane again, the sound echoing through the room. She glared at the three matriarchs. "*Enough,* both of you. If I can tolerate having all three of you under my roof for one evening, you can all be civil to one another."

"All *three* of us?" the elder Talbot grumbled. "I'll thank you not to lump us in with them. *We* haven't done anything."

"Oh, shut it, Eleanor Talbot. I know you're just waiting for your chance to dig up some old trouble."

Eleanor Talbot scowled, but Victoria caught a twinkle in her eye. She put a restraining hand on Hannah's shoulder, warning the younger woman against whatever she was about to say. Maledicta nodded, satisfied, then glared around the room.

"Hear me now. You're in *my* home. That wasn't my idea, but Wilhelmina left me a tidy sum in exchange for hosting you here. You're all going to go into my drawing room, sit well away from one another, and let Morry divide up whatever she's left to you all. Then you can all go back to trying to kill one another *after* you leave. If anyone has a problem with that, the door is behind you."

"Mistress Bruttenholm's instructions were quite clear," Gray added in his lugubrious voice. "To receive a bequest, beneficiaries *must* fulfill her final wishes, which are only to be delivered tonight, in this place." He patted the breast of his suit. "And only I have her final wishes."

The mistresses of Ravenkirk stared at each other, waiting to see who would leave. No one moved. Greed, or just plain curiosity, overrode their obvious distaste for one another. Maledicta nodded in satisfaction.

"There we are, then. Let's all go into the drawing room so

Morry can get this show on the road and all of you out of my house. Everyone, kindly keep the bloodshed to a minimum, hmm?"

A murmur of assent rippled through the lobby. Maledicta formed the head of the line as everyone began filing toward the drawing room. The people didn't seem chastened, exactly, but the mood struck Victoria as less openly combative.

Then Maledicta threw open the door to the drawing room and Abigail Gilman let out a blood-curdling scream.

There, in the middle of the floor, lay Bianca Burke, staring up at the ceiling in a pool of her own blood. Her throat had been slashed from ear to ear.

It took an hour to get everyone calmed. The Talbots, Gilmans, and Ruthvens immediately fell to blaming one another. Specifically, the Talbots and Gilmans pointed fingers at Nicodemus. The Ruthven matriarch angrily defended her nephew, hurling imprecations at the other families. The shouting went round and round for the first half hour, the same accusations tossed like knives without pause.

Maledicta tried to referee, thumping her cane on the floor and reminding the feuding families that this was still *her* house, dammit, and she was going to have quiet. That did no good. Dolores Ruthven rounded on her, pointing out nastily that it *was* her home, and didn't that make her a likely suspect, and they were all off to the races again.

The only ones currently above suspicion were Tabitha's group and Victoria herself. Victoria wasn't part of any long-standing grudges and obviously had no motive. Tabitha and company were Wilhelmina's employees or something. Presumably that made them heir to whatever grudges held against her, but it seemed everyone would rather score points off a live target.

Victoria couldn't stand all the noise. It was hard enough seeing Bianca's body sprawled across the floor, her blue eyes staring blankly at nothing, her blood slowly spreading in a wide puddle. She'd never seen a dead body like this, let alone someone she knew and sort of liked. The screaming—well, that brought back bad memories of its own. She wanted to flee, out the front door or up to her room, but had enough presence of mind to recognize that would only make her look guilty. It was only a matter of time before they stopped pointing fingers at one another and turned on the outsider.

Seeing her distress, Thorn peeled off from their group and gently took Victoria by the arm. They led her into the kitchen and sat her on a stool in the corner. Then they left her alone for a bit while they bustled around in the cabinets.

Victoria sat slumped on the stool, staring at the black and gray tile floor. She wasn't really sure what was going on. She wasn't even certain what room she was in or how she'd gotten there. She was glad that it was quiet now and the floor was clean. She admired the dark swirls in the tiles beneath her feet, the patterns they made, the fact that they were entirely blood-free.

A shadow fell over her. She looked up in time to see Thorn place a cardboard box in her lap. The violet-haired femme gave her a lopsided smile.

"Figured you'd like to see her. Take your mind off things."

Victoria opened the box. Samantha looked up, waving a front leg. Victoria put her hand in the box and the tarantula skittered up it, climbing her arm until she rested on Victoria's shoulder. She huddled by Victoria's neck, almost as if she was cuddling her. Victoria could almost swear she heard the tarantula purr. Tarantulas didn't do that, did they?

"You got a preference for tea?" Thorn asked. "Because I was just going to brew some Constant Comment."

Victoria stared at them, uncomprehending, until the whistling kettle broke her reverie. She blinked three times, quickly. Thorn had put a pot on to make tea. They were offering her a cup. That sounded fantastic right now.

"That's... that would be great," Victoria said. After a second, she remembered to add, "Thank you."

Thorn smiled and fixed her a cup, then handed it over with a small plate of shortbread cookies. Victoria thought she was too upset to eat, until the first nibble. She ate two cookies before she even realized it. Thorn gave her an approving smile.

"Good girl," they said, sending a wave of warmth through Victoria's abdomen. "You sit and settle. I'll just poke my head out and see if anyone... if the shouting's still going on."

Victoria nodded. Covering her face, she said around a mouthful of shortbread, "I thought guests weren't allowed in the kitchen."

Thorn winked. "The Dread Mistress is busy, so I'm in charge."

Before they could leave the room, the door flew open.

Tzipporah rushed in, closing the door behind her. From her expression, she didn't bring good news. Thorn groaned.

"Oh Hell, what now?"

"Bad news and worse," Tzipporah said.

"Feels like that kind of night."

Tzipporah nodded at Victoria, sharing a sort of sympathy, then turned back to Thorn. "The mood's bad out there. The shouting had about died down. Then the sheriff showed up."

Thorn groaned. "That was quick."

"There *was* a murder."

"Yeah, but on Maledicta's property. That ought to mean something."

Tzipporah shrugged.

"So I guess the Abbey's a crime scene now?" Thorn laughed mirthlessly. "I'm sure the Dread Mistress is happy about that."

Tzipporah rolled her eyes. "Please. You know Her Darkness would never stand for that. Alison's already mopping up the blood."

Thorn looked confused. "Wait, what about Burke's body?"

Tzipporah glanced at Victoria. "See, that's what I was coming to tell you …"

Before she could say anything else, the kitchen door banged open again. The two Talbot men came in, carrying Bianca's body between them. Victoria jumped off the stool, nearly dropping her mug and shrieking. Only the warmth radiating from Samantha kept her calm.

She still might have lost it, had someone not thoughtfully

wrapped a dark red handkerchief around Bianca's neck.

A balding man in a khaki police uniform, utterly forgettable except for his meticulously polished badge, followed the three in. He glanced around the room, trying to project far more gravitas than he deserved, one hand on the butt of his service pistol. He locked eyes with Thorn, who glared at him as if he was a cockroach who'd just scuttled into their clean kitchen. The sheriff flinched but didn't back down. Possibly because of the crush of people gathered just outside the open door.

"Muh… Mih… ah, Hale," he said. "I need you to open up the walk-in so we can store Miss Burke until the cold car arrives."

Thorn's eyes blazed. "You want to store a dead body in *my* freezer?"

The sheriff's ruddy face paled. "Now, now, just until morning. Morgue's closed already, you know that. Hell, you're lucky I came out here at all, ayuh."

Thorn looked like they were about to tell the man where he could stick it when Maledicta shoved past him. She waved a ringed hand at him, gesturing for silence. The sheriff fumed at being so casually dismissed but didn't say anything.

"It's *my* freezer, Thorn," Maledicta said, sounding weary, "and *I* said to keep her remains safe and cool until we can handle them properly. She's still a guest of the Abbey, and the Abbey will take care of her."

Tzipporah looked helplessly at Thorn and shrugged. Thorn was mad enough to spit nails, but moved aside so the Talbots could carry Bianca to the freezer. She gave Victoria an apologetic look before opening it up.

"If all this fuss has been settled," Gray said from the doorway, "we can resume the night's events. If you'll all join me in the drawing room, we'll begin the will reading shortly."

Victoria stared at him, open-mouthed. "Are you *joking?* Bianca was *murdered.* Are you going to act like nothing happened?"

"The authorities were summoned, Ms. Williams." Gray nodded to the sheriff, who looked like a dog caught between multiple masters. "The investigation has begun, and I have every confidence justice will be done. In the *morning*. In the meantime, I have duties of my own to conduct. If you'll come this way?"

"I can't believe this. I'm not going to a *will reading* tonight. Not in the same room a woman was killed in!"

Gray cocked his head to one side. "Are you forfeiting your bequest, then?"

"Excuse me?"

"Ms. Williams, I thought I made the situation perfectly clear. Mistress Bruttenholm's final instructions were unmistakable and *inviolable*. The will reading is to be conducted *tonight* and *in person*. Any beneficiary not present when I read their bequest will forfeit it." He withdrew a heavy antique pocket watch and looked at the time with a deep frown. "We barely have three hours to meet the requirements. I suggest everyone move *quickly*."

Victoria looked around the room incredulously, trying to find some support, someone to help her make some *sense* of this. There was none forthcoming. Her eyes found Thorn's, still standing beside the open freezer. They shrugged, resigned.

The Talbot men exited the freezer. Thorn shut the door with an ominous *thud*. It sounded of finality and inevitability. The Talbots filed out of the kitchen, following Gray and Maledicta. Thorn and Tzipporah fell in line behind them, looking at Victoria expectantly.

Victoria swore under her breath and hopped off the stool, letting Samantha's empty box tumble onto the floor.

She was the last to enter the drawing room. Alison was directing traffic, showing the different families to their own clusters of chairs. The matriarchs had clearly brought more relations than the Abbey had anticipated; Tzipporah had fetched a dozen steel folding chairs and was setting them up for the Talbots and Gilmans. The Talbot men, noticeably large on the steel chairs, didn't look especially comfortable, but then, Tzipporah didn't look especially concerned.

Alison guided Victoria to her own seat, a lone chair off to the right. She was independent of the town's factions, of course, and had no entourage other than Samantha. Alison didn't say anything about the spider riding Victoria's shoulder. Victoria herself had entirely forgotten about Samantha until she realized Nicodemus was staring at them.

The younger Ruthven sat on the other side of the drawing room, alone save for the teenager Victoria desperately hoped was a younger sister or cousin. She didn't appear too happy about being forced to sit in a steel chair. Nicodemus paid her no mind. He was more interested in Victoria and her spider.

"That looks rather familiar." He leered, looking at her over the tops of his shades. "Good to see you're getting along well."

"Samantha and I are getting along splendidly," Victoria said to no one in particular.

She put her hand to her shoulder, letting Samantha crawl on it. Victoria moved the tarantula down into her lap, where she turned around three times before settling. She had to resist the urge to stroke her abdomen – she knew it was delicate, and likely to have irritating hairs – and instead set one hand very close to Samantha's front legs. Samantha put one leg on Victoria's pinkie and left it there.

Nicodemus was still smirking at her. The teenager was glaring at Victoria now, clearly upset that Nicodemus was paying attention to someone else. Victoria suppressed a sigh, instead looking at the portrait of Wilhelmina Bruttenholm propped up by the table. She wondered what exactly the old woman found so amusing. Did she think all of this was funny from beyond the grave? Was Victoria just an unwilling part of a post-mortem prank?

She didn't have time to ponder that further, for Gray stepped up to the table. He clapped his hands once, making a noise like sandpaper-covered twigs breaking. The others fell silent, every eye in the room fixed on him. He smiled thinly, as if relishing the moment. Then he set his briefcase on the table and opened it, withdrawing a scroll wrapped in burgundy ribbon. It had been sealed in black wax, a stylized "B" stamped in the middle. Gray broke the seal with his thumb and unfurled the scroll. Clearing his throat dramatically, he began to read.

"I, Wilhelmina Johanna Bruttenholm, being of sound mind if steadily failing body, do hereby make my last will and testament. I have watched over the town of Ravenkirk my whole life. I have watched over *you* my whole life, and it has been a long and tumultuous one. I have witnessed your secrets, your lies, and your sins. Some of those I have sworn to take to my grave. Some of those you still believe are hidden.

"I was unable to prevent you from turning my beloved home into the playground for your many tawdry grudges. Perhaps I was not strong enough, nor brave enough. Perhaps I simply feared what would happen if I took one side or the other.

"Now, I am gone, and my personal weaknesses will no longer stay my hand.

"I have amassed much over the years. Knowledge and secrets and artifacts and of course, base coin. A portion will go to each of you, provided you fulfill my final wishes.

"I hope this bequest sets some of you free.

"I hope this bequest destroys the rest of you.

"Signed by my hand on this date, September 22nd, Two Thousand Twenty-Two, Wilhelmina Bruttenholm."

"Almost exactly a year ago," Abigail Gilman muttered.

Lavinia scoffed. "Overly dramatic old hag."

Eleanor Talbot twisted in her seat, glaring at the Ruthven woman. "Some respect for the dead, young lady. Lord knows you have little enough for the living."

"Or what?" Lavinia said, uncowed. "Is a show of respect a requirement in the old bat's will?"

"It is not," Gray said, his lugubrious voice rumbling with disapproval, "though one might consider it a requirement of *propriety.*"

Lavinia rolled her eyes and folded her arms but didn't antagonize him any further. Gray set the will down and withdrew the contents of his suit's inner pocket. He held a dozen sealed envelopes, each addressed to a specific person in calligraphy.

"In accordance with Mistress Bruttenholm's instructions, which I have available should anyone wish to inspect them, I shall open these letters in their prescribed order. I will read their public contents, then provide any bequest along with the private letter. If anyone would like to confirm these are Mistress Bruttenholm's direct instructions?"

Gray withdrew a sheet of paper from the briefcase. He showed a neatly typed block of text with a looping signature and notary seal at the bottom. No one seemed to want to object. After giving them exactly one minute to consider, he nodded in satisfaction and began.

"The first letter is addressed to Ms. Victoria Williams." He slid the envelope open and unfolded its contents.

*Dear Ms. Williams,*

*You are no doubt confused by your presence, both here and at the front of the list. Let me reassure you that first, no, you do not know me, nor have we ever met. Second, much will become clear after you read the packet of information I have prepared for you. Thank you for humoring an old woman. I promise to make it worth your while.*

*In exchange for fulfilling the task I have set for you, I hereby bequeath you a sum of two million dollars—*

A gasp leapt across the room. Victoria's hand flew to her mouth. Gray ignored them, pressing on.

*"—to be delivered upon confirmation of completion. Until such time, the money will be held in trust. As you will need to remain in Ravenkirk until your task is complete, you will receive a weekly stipend of one thousand dollars, to be administered by my executor.*

*To help with your task, I also bequeath the contents of this wooden box, labeled with your name.*

*Yours in mystery, Wilhelmina Bruttenholm."*

Victoria stared in shock as Gray handed her the letter, a small wooden box and a manilla envelope, all marked with her name in Wilhelmina's fine script. Samantha shifted slightly, giving the old lawyer a space to lay the material in her lap. As he turned away, she finally found her voice.

"What am I supposed to do with this?"

He looked over his skinny shoulder and shrugged. "Read it, I suppose. I would recommend you start with the files. They might offer more context."

Numb, she opened the manilla envelope and looked inside. Her face fell when she saw its contents.

"Hey, what gives?"

Gray was wrong. There were no records inside the folder, no files, no answers. Just a three-year-old fashion magazine. A celebrity she didn't recognize smiled blandly back at her, teeth too rigid, pores and wrinkles erased by photo manipulation.

The lawyer stared at the magazine in shock. Somehow even more color drained from his already bloodless face. He snatched it from her hand, glaring impotently at the slick cover.

"That cannot be," he stammered.

He dropped the magazine and dashed to the file boxes, pulling them out one at a time and examining their contents. One in three had been tampered with, their contents replaced by years-old periodicals.

Tabitha appeared over Victoria's shoulder, mouth grim.

"I think we know why Bianca was murdered," she said.

## 09

Victoria didn't wait around for the rest of the reading. As soon as there was a lull in the shouting, she slipped out and ran upstairs. Her room was small and cold, but it was also quiet, and more importantly, *hers*.

She fell onto her bed for what felt like hours, waiting for the hubbub downstairs to die down. Snatches of shouted accusations still floated up through the vents. She was grateful to be out of it. She wondered if all will readings were like this. She'd never known anyone with enough assets to actually have one before.

Of course, as Wilhelmina admitted, Victoria hadn't known her either. A complete stranger had left her two million dollars. Two million dollars? Two *million* dollars. That wasn't as much as it used to be, but it was certainly more than she'd ever imagined having at one time. She wouldn't be set for life, but hell, even after taxes that was enough to be very comfortable. She could pay off her student loans. Throw away her credit cards. Not worry about paying for HRT for a long, long time.

Oh God, she could maybe buy a house!

All Victoria had to do was fulfill one simple task. She ought to find out what it was. As the shouting finally died away and the last of Ravenkirk's great and good filed out of Huntingdon Abbey, Victoria opened Wilhelmina's private letter and began to read.

*Dear Ms. Williams,*

*I imagine you have more questions. I hope the records I left to you answer some of them. I hope it does you good to learn where your parents came from.*

Victoria glanced at the fashion magazine, lying open on the bare floorboards, and rolled her eyes.

*Many in Ravenkirk believe that with family comes obligations. If you knew anything about the Bruttenholms, you would understand how I laugh at that sentiment. The task I set before you is a difficult one, and one that calls to your lost family name. Nonetheless, it is not a burden you should feel obligated to pick up. Hence, why I left you the greater part of my own fortune.*

*I love this town, Ms. Williams. Despite its flaws and petty sins, I have loved it all my life, and I have sought to protect it. I hope, after today, that you love it too.*

*I hope my apprentices will take up the task of protecting it. Please, Ms. Williams, help them. You may feel like an outsider here. You may feel that you are out of your depth. I assure you that you aren't. You may be the only one who can save Ravenkirk from itself.*

*In the box I left you, you will find a key. It opens a chest, hidden generations ago by one of your ancestors. Retrieve the treasure within and your task is complete. After that, I can only hope you will know what to do.*

*I know this is vague, Ms. Williams, but were I to explain more at this point, you would dismiss it as an old woman's fancy. I assure you, everything you will shortly learn is true.*

*Yours,*

*Wilhelmina Bruttenholm*

Victoria dropped the letter and picked up the box. It was hard wood, stained a brown so dark it was nearly black. Someone had engraved a symbol at the top; presumably it was the Bruttenholm family seal, or at least Wilhelmina's. It was a gothic "B" superimposed over a tall oval, surmounting an owl with spread wings. Victoria brushed her fingertips across it, feeling the dips in the wood. It gave her goosebumps. She felt as if she stood inside an open doorway, wondering if she dared to cross the threshold.

Taking a deep breath, she grabbed the lid and flipped it open.

She was disappointed to see it was, in fact, just a key. In fairness, it was an ornate, antique key. The barrel was brass, about three inches long. The teeth were pointed, like the tines of a crown, or perhaps the curved fangs of a monster. The head was flat and heart-shaped, with a skull stamped on the side. A tiny red gem sparkled in a skull's left eye socket.

Disappointment swiftly gave way to curiosity. This was no mere tchotchke. It was the start of a mystery; one Wilhelmina was daring her to solve.

Victoria read the letter again and again, trying to force it to make sense, knowing that was impossible without Wilhelmina's missing files. It didn't add up. Despite what Wilhelmina Bruttenholm believed, Victoria's family had no connection to Ravenkirk, at least as far as she knew. Her parents had lived in Boston their entire lives. So had their parents.

Unless they hadn't? She realized she had no way of knowing. Mom was dead and Dad might as well be; she hadn't heard from him since elementary school. Aunt Agatha was the one living relative she knew, and they weren't on speaking terms since Victoria's transition.

She flung her arm over her face, dropped the pages on the floor and let out a moan.

"Come on. Someone give me an actual answer."

Something scraped at the window. She ignored it. The storm was shaking the trees, making their branches scratch at the Abbey. The staff ought to trim them.

Maybe she should just leave tomorrow like she'd planned. Sure, she'd be giving up a lot of money, but someone had already been killed over it. Bianca was dead, and no one seemed particularly concerned about that. One murdered outsider was less important than whatever they hoped to get out of Wilhelmina's estate. It was ghoulish.

Samantha skittered up her leg, crawling along until she settled on Victoria's stomach. Her eight jewel-like eyes glittered at Victoria. The girl sighed and put out her hand for the tarantula to climb on.

"It's kind of chilly up here, Samantha. You sure you wouldn't be happier downstairs?"

Unsurprisingly, Samantha didn't say anything. She just sat on Victoria's hand, gently vibrating. Victoria was certain the tarantula was purring now.

The branches scratched the window again. Victoria turned her head toward the curtain. The storm must be getting bad. She hoped the glass was strong enough. The last thing she needed was a tree limb flying through her room on top of everything else.

Wait, was there even a tree on this side of the building?

Before she could get up to check, the glass shattered. Wood smashed through the window and whipped the curtain aside, but it wasn't a tree branch. It was an arm, covered in flannel, stuffed with straw and tipped with sharp wooden fingers. A scarecrow clambered through the window, its burlap face twisted into a rictus grin.

Victoria screamed and fell off the bed, Samatha skittering away to safety. She scooted backwards on her ass, bumping up against the too-near wall. The scarecrow crawled across the bed on all fours, like a beast. It stopped when it saw the key on the floor, where it had landed when Victoria fell. Wooden fingers closed around it, black thread grin widening.

"That's mine," Victoria said weakly. "That's mine!"

The scarecrow's head jerked around, like a dog scenting prey. An eerie light flickered in the burlap folds of its eyes. It keened, the eerie sound welling up from within its overstuffed body. Sitting back, it prepared to pounce.

Then it jerked its arm in what looked impossibly like pain. Samantha clung to its flannel sleeve, fangs sunk into the fabric. The flannel smoked where she bit, a rotten black patch spreading from it across the scarecrow's arm. It flailed, limb unraveling, wooden fingers clattering to the floor with the key. Samantha leapt, skittering away from the scarecrow's stomping boots.

"You leave her alone!" Victoria shouted.

She threw herself at the scarecrow, shoving it hard. The monster fell against the bed, lashing out with one boot. It caught Victoria in the stomach, knocking the wind out of her. She fell, gasping for breath. She at least had the presence of mind to grab the key. Samantha hid under the bed, eight legs shaking.

A hard fist pounded on the door. The scarecrow paused, one arm raised to tear open Victoria's back. The fist pounded on the door again, harder. It fell inward, slamming to the floor with a loud *bang*. Bianca stood in the doorway, a blood-stained bandana around her torn throat, a bandage over her left eye, and blood soaked into her frost-stiff jumpsuit. She was even paler than before. That made sense, in Victoria's dazed mind. The last time Victoria had seen her, all of her blood had leaked out onto the drawing room floor.

The scarecrow leapt at the new target, claws out. Bianca

caught its good arm and slammed it against the wall. She slammed an elbow into its throat, pinning it to the wall, grabbed its burlap head with her other hand, and pulled. The sack head came free of its neck with a sound like flesh tearing. Victoria half-expected a gout of human blood to follow. Instead, a puff of green smoke escaped the open collar.

Bianca let the remains fall to the floor. They landed with a soft thump, once again just a pile of old clothes stuffed with straw. She stood over Victoria, offering a blood-stained hand.

"Come on." Her voice was low and raspy. "We need to get you out of here."

Victoria stared at her, mind numb. The only thing she could think to say was, "That's not the line."

Bianca cocked her head to one side, staring at Victoria with her good eye. "What?"

"The line. It's, 'Come with me if you want to live'."

"Ladybug, what the fuck are you talking about?"

"Nothing." She took Bianca's hand. It was uncomfortably cold. "Bianca, you're dead."

Bianca hauled Victoria to her feet, unbothered by the weight. "Bianca. Is that my name?"

Victoria's heart sank. "Oh no."

A scream came from downstairs. Bianca's head jerked around, tracking the threat. "We don't have time for this. Run."

Bianca didn't wait for her to respond. She took off running, pulling Victoria along down the hall and to the stairs. They found the sound of the scream on the second-floor landing—another scarecrow stood over the body of a sheriff's deputy, his throat and stomach torn open by wooden claws. Bianca launched herself at the effigy, shouting for Victoria to keep running. Victoria did as she was told, flying down the stairs and into the claws of another waiting monster. The third scarecrow lurked in the doorway to the ground-floor hallway. She fell backward as it swiped at her, narrowly avoiding its claws and landing butt-first on the stairs. The scarecrow loomed over her, ready to strike.

Then something whistled in the air and the tip of a crossbow bolt appeared in the middle of its face. Green smoke leaked out around the bolt. The effigy fell to its knees and collapsed in on itself. Behind it stood Tabitha, reloading her crossbow.

"It's been a shit night," she said. "You okay, sweetheart?"

"I've been better," Victoria said quietly.

"Same," Bianca said above her.

Bianca came down the stairs, holding the second scarecrow's burlap head. She dropped it, letting it roll down the stairs to join the body of the third. Tabitha looked startled to see her but recovered smoothly.

"Ms. Burke," she said, not lowering her crossbow. "You're back on your feet."

"And someone's going to regret that, I can fucking promise you that," Bianca said through gritted teeth. "But first, we have to get Ladybug to safety."

"This place ought to *be* safe."

Thorn emerged from the library, looking disheveled. They were bleeding from long scratches down their bare arms. Their gloved hands were smoking and soot stained.

"Something's possessing the scarecrows outside the Abbey. They sent them to attack us." Thorn shook their head. "That shouldn't be possible. The Abbey is warded against malevolent spirits."

"Not just the Abbey," Tabitha said. "We've got reports of attacks all across town. Drake is at the town square. Megan's protecting the docks."

"The Gilmans will love that," Thorn said sourly.

"I couldn't give a fuck what the Gilmans think about anything, especially right now. We have bigger things to worry about."

"Such as?"

"Someone must have weakened the wards," Tabitha said. "There are only a handful of people who could have done that."

"Don't say it," Thorn snapped. "For all I know it was one of your crew. You've always rejected the Abbey's support. Are you afraid? Now that you don't have a patron?"

Tabitha bristled. She and Thorn squared off, Tabitha fingering her crossbow's trigger, Thorn spreading their hands wide. Without thinking, Victoria jumped between them.

"Stop it, both of you!" She looked back and forth between them, giving both a stern glare. "Look, I don't know what's going on except that monsters are attacking *all* of us. How is fighting each other going to help?"

Tabitha and Thorn stared at Victoria, then at each other. They eyed one another warily. Then Thorn gave Tabitha a lopsided grin. They put their hands in their pockets while Tabitha lowered her crossbow.

"You know who it probably was?" they said.

Tabitha nodded, realization dawning. "Nicodemus."

"Fucking Nicodemus."

Victoria was confused for a second, not wanting to believe the implications. "So, Nicodemus Ruthven is, what, some sort of *wizard?*"

Tabitha nodded. "Something like that."

Thorn snickered. "Welcome to Ravenkirk."

Victoria looked over her shoulder at the dead woman shadowing her. It was absurd, but she'd seen plenty of absurd in the past fifteen minutes. Magic was real and so were monsters. Well, why not? Her stomach still hurt where the scarecrow had kicked her. Disbelieving wouldn't make that stop.

Bianca stepped forward, putting a hand on Victoria's shoulder. "Why would Nicodemus Ruthven want to hurt Victoria?"

Thorn gestured to the lacerations on their arms. "He didn't *just* want to hurt *her.*"

"But I *was* a target. One of them came into my room." She opened her hand, showing them the key. "It was trying to get this. Wilhelmina left it to me. It has something to do with what she wants me to do."

Tabitha turned to her, eyes full of sorrow and curiosity. "What was that?"

Victoria was about to answer, but Bianca's grip on her shoulder tightened, silencing her. "That's not important right now. This place isn't safe. We have to get her somewhere that is."

Thorn looked like they wanted to object, but Tabitha interrupted them.

"The bookstore. It's still secure, as far as I know." She flashed Thorn a smug look. "Nicodemus' lifetime ban still stands there."

Thorn rolled their eyes. "*My* boss wasn't the one who summoned the fucker home."

"Enough. We move."

Not waiting for the others to respond, Bianca took Victoria by the arm—surprisingly gently, for her newfound strength—and led her down the hall. Tabitha and Thorn hurried behind, neither wanting to be left out. Mercy was outside with a big bag of salt, dumping it in a wide circle around the grounds. She startled when they called her name, dropping the bag and yelling in fright.

"The wards are damaged!" she shouted.

"We know, and there's no time to fix them," Thorn shouted back. "We're all getting out of here before there's another attack."

Mercy looked confused, but followed Thorn to their car, leaving the bag where it fell. Bianca went straight to her sportscar, only to stop before opening the door.

"What's wrong?" Victoria asked.

Bianca frowned. "I don't... I don't remember how to drive."

Tabitha jerked a thumb at her truck. "There's only room for two of you in that car anyway. Come on."

Victoria and Bianca piled into Tabitha's truck. A few hours ago, Victoria would have been thrilled to be squished in such a close space between these two women. Now, she was frightened out of her mind and uncomfortably aware of how cold Bianca was. As Tabitha drove, Victoria kept sneaking glances at Bianca, who simply stared straight ahead. Her expression was unreadable, in part because the eye facing Victoria was covered in a bandage. Two runners of blood ran around it, drying in crusty trails.

"Why are you doing this, Bianca?" Victoria asked, her voice low and soft.

Bianca whipped her head around, fixing Victoria with her good eye. Angry red lines shot through the sclera, but the iris was unnervingly blue. Victoria tried to hide it, but Bianca's gaze made her shiver.

"It's my job." Bianca turned her gaze back to the road.

"It's all she can remember," Tabitha said, mostly to herself. "Her last job. Protecting you."

Bianca didn't respond. She simply stared out the window, colorless lips set in a grim line.

"Wilhelmina must have left you a hell of a retainer," Victoria mumbled.

Bianca's head dropped to her chest. He pressed her fists against the hollow of her throat and mumbled, "To pay your way."

Victoria burned with questions, but she feared the answers. Walking scarecrows, pretty gals back from the dead, witches and wizards and who knew what else? Even Samantha—she had no idea what sort of tarantula had a mark like a skull on her abdomen, let alone venom that tore apart monsters. Before she could come up with the first thing to ask, Tabitha brought the truck to a sudden stop.

"Shit."

They were about a block from the bookstore. It was a two-story building; the first floor sported a large plate window, the second a tall, gabled roof with two dormers. Nicodemus Ruthven leaned against the locked front door. He turned his head to stare at the truck, smiling nastily.

Thorn's car stopped behind them. Thorn and Mercy climbed out, slowly walking up the street toward him. Tabitha warned Victoria to stay in the truck. Then she hopped out, unlimbering her crossbow. Bianca patted Victoria on the knee and followed Tabitha.

Nicodemus pushed off the door and took a few steps toward the others, hands in his coat pockets. Tabitha raised her crossbow and shouted at him to show his hands and stay put. Wonder of wonders, he obeyed, although the sardonic grin never left his face. Thorn and Bianca circled around him, trying to keep him fenced in.

Mercy fell back to the truck. She yanked open the passenger door and grabbed Victoria's wrist. "Come on!"

Victoria pulled back. "What are you doing?"

"You don't want to be sitting here if Nicodemus decides to put up a fight." Mercy's voice was a harsh hiss. "Which he *will*. Come *on!*"

Nicodemus stood in the middle of the street, the others forming a rough triangle around him. Something about his expression made it clear he didn't feal threatened. He was saying something, but too low for Victoria to make out over the truck's engine. Something about it made Tabitha's hand twitch. Fearing for the worst, Victoria allowed Mercy to pull her out of the cab and down the nearest alley. Mercy led her halfway down before ducking behind a half-full dumpster.

"What do we do now?" Victoria whispered.

"Now I finish what I started."

Before Victoria could ask Mercy what she meant, the other woman whipped around and jammed a fist into her stomach. Victoria let out a gasp as a sharp pain forced all the air out of her lungs. She looked down to see a long knife protruding from her abdomen, stabbing up under her ribcage.

She couldn't call for help. She couldn't even ask why.

Mercy grabbed her shoulder and shoved. Victoria fell back, the knife slipping out of her stomach and unleashing a gout of blood. Boneless, she collapsed on the dirty alley floor. The key fell from her nerveless fingers, clattering across the asphalt. Mercy bent down to scoop it up, then ran.

Victoria tried to turn in the direction Mercy had gone, tried to call for help. She couldn't do either. All she could manage was to stare up at the dark sky as the darkness swallowed her.

**10**

If anyone had asked, Victoria would have said she had no idea what the afterlife was like, that she wasn't even sure there was one. If pressed, she'd say she hoped it was full of attractive women in corsets and amazing eye makeup. That would have been a joke, mostly. It wasn't a subject she'd ever thought about a lot, especially once she started her transition. She'd been too busy realizing she wanted to live.

If cornered at a party and forced to give a real answer, she certainly never would have suggested the hereafter looked like the interior of an empty mansion, lit only by an eerie pink light that seeped through the dusty windows. Yet, when she opened her eyes, there she was. Sprawled on her back in a spreading pool of blood, chest aching where the knife had gone in, staring up at a dark vaulted ceiling.

She was dead and it still hurt. That wasn't fair.

Victoria put a ginger hand to her chest, wincing as she touched the stab wound. It didn't appear to be bleeding. That was good. Unless it meant all the blood had poured out of her. That made a lot of sense, actually.

"This wasn't how I expected this weekend to go," she said to no one in particular.

"Neither did I," said another voice in the gloom.

Victoria's head snapped around. Wilhelmina Bruttenholm stepped out of the shadows, her face both stern and sad. She wore the same dark coat as Tabitha and carried an iron lantern. A pale flame danced within it, occasionally taking the form of a tiny naked woman with backswept horns, other times a little lizard with eight legs and a wide mouth. An owl perched on her shoulder, glowing with silver light.

"Am I actually seeing a ghost, or is my dying brain just throwing random bullshit at me?" Victoria asked.

Wilhelmina set the lantern down on the bare boards. She squatted next to Victoria, elbows on her knees, a knowing smirk on her face. The owl cocked their head to one side, wide eyes fixed on Victoria, and hooted once. It sounded like a funeral bell.

"I'm afraid I don't know you well enough to guess which you'd prefer to hear," she said. "Not that I've ever been in the business of telling folks what they *want* to hear. This is what you *need* to hear. You're dying. You aren't dead yet, but my team won't reach you in time to save you, and Nicodemus is too interested in blood to be any help."

An icy chill gripped Victoria's heart. Was it fear, or was her broken body already giving up the ghost? She struggled to sit up, grabbing for Wilhelmina's hand, hoping it would be substantial enough to give her some comfort.

"Please, Miss Bruttenholm, you *have* to *help me!*"

Wilhelmina snatched her hand back, as if it was too near a fire. "I'm trying, honey. There's not much I can do right now."

"Not much…?" Something inside Victoria snapped. She raged at the ghost, the mansion's wooden walls shivered through her tears. "What's going *on?* What am I even *doing* here? I'm *dying*. A stranger *murdered* me and I don't even know *why!*"

Wilhelmina ducked her head, looking genuinely apologetic. "I'm sorry. I tried to give you the truth. I wasn't expecting someone to steal it."

Victoria stared at her, shoulders shaking. "Well, I'm here now, aren't I? Not much else going on. You could just *tell* me."

The Owl hooted, a dolorous peal marking the ending of her life. Wilhelmina glanced at them, cross.

"I *know* I can't tell her that," she snapped. She looked back at Victoria, her face softening. "I'm sorry, dear. There are rules to this sort of thing. I've crossed the veil; I'm out of the game now. I can't tell you why I brought you here, not now."

The Owl hooted again, more insistently. Wilhelmina sighed heavily and offered her hand, palm out.

"Unless you choose to come with us, of course. Then I can answer every question I have an answer for."

Understanding fell upon Victoria like a lead tablet. "But I'll be dead."

"That's right."

"So I won't be able to *do* anything about it."

"Right again."

A frown creased Victoria's brow. "Bianca's dead. She seems to be doing plenty about it."

The Owl bristled, feathers sticking out every which way as they flapped their wings and spun their head. A sound like metal grinding on metal echoed across the room. Wilhelmina grimaced, shaking her head.

"Yeah, and I'm going to have to talk with *someone* about that." She shook her head. "Different rules. Believe me, you *don't* want to take the deal Ms. Burke took."

Victoria pulled her hand away. "Then what deal *should* I take?"

"Now *there's* a question I can answer. Sort of." Wilhelmina stood, spectral knees somehow popping. "I can't tell you which deal to take, but I can tell you there's some folks coming to help you, after a fashion." Her voice trailed off, sounding like it was coming from a long ways away. "If it's advice you want, have some for free. *Listen* to what they're offering and understand the price."

"That's it?" Victoria stared, incredulous. "*Caveat emptor*, that's all you've got for me?"

Wilhelmina was fading. She grinned, satisfied. "It's good advice, missy. Take it or leave it."

Before Victoria could reply, Mistress Bruttenholm was gone, although the iron lantern stayed behind. She stared into the pale green flame, watching the tiny dancer. She shivered. The flame gave off no heat, and Victoria was getting colder. That couldn't be a good sign.

She wasn't alone in the dark for long. A mist rose around her, carrying a faint stench of sulfur. A tall man in a black coat stepped out of the shadows. There was something goatish about him. He had a long face surrounded by a dark beard, and his eyes glowed eerily. When he reached his thin hand up to stroke his beard, Victoria saw a heavy emerald ring on one finger, the massive jewel set in silver. Something dark swirled within it.

"We finally meet, Victoria," he said, his voice deep like an empty grave. He offered her his other hand. "Come along. You don't have much time."

Victoria pulled back. There was something about this man she didn't trust. Maybe it was the way he leered at her, as if she was a wayward pet he'd finally tracked down. Maybe it was the eagerness with which he reached for her hand. Or perhaps it was just the stench of brimstone that clung to him like a wealthy woman's perfume.

"I don't know who you are," she said, "but I'm not going anywhere with you. I don't even know your name."

"My name?" The stranger smiled, revealing wide, flat teeth. "I've had so many over the years. They collect like cobwebs in the corners. It isn't important what men call me. What's important is that you come home, before it's too late."

The stranger came closer. Victoria scooted back, smearing blood across the bare boards. He knelt, putting his fingers in the pool of blood. Raising his bloody hand to his face, he sniffed them, then ran his tongue over his fingers. He smiled, satisfied.

"You've lost an awful lot of blood, Victoria. How much more do you think you can afford to lose?"

"My friends are coming." She didn't sound convincing even to herself.

"And what do you think they'll do, exactly?" The stranger sneered. "*If* they reach you before you bleed out, what are they going to do? Call for an ambulance? You'll be dead before it arrives. Stitch you up? Pour their own blood into you? Don't be absurd. They can't help you."

"Oh, but you can?"

He leaned forward, one hand on his knee, the other pressed against the floor next to her hip. His long face loomed over her. She thought she might gag at the brimstone stench.

"That's right. I can make your body whole again. I can do so much more. All you have to do is ask."

Victoria turned her face away, trying desperately to breathe fresh air. "And I suppose you'll do that out of the kindness of your heart."

The stranger's leering grin widened. "Of course I won't. But who among us can put a price on life?"

He held out his hand. "Your time grows short. Come away, now."

Victoria felt her hand lifting of its own accord. She didn't reach for him. Not yet. He was too greedy, too clearly hungry for her. At the same time, she didn't know what else to do. He was right about one thing; she could feel herself getting weaker, her heart slowing. What other choice did she have?

The answer came in the sound of a crashing wave. A harsh voice rang out from behind her. "Not so fast, you old goat!"

A large woman came striding out of the shadows, her thick form wrapped in a seawater-soaked robe. She was wide-hipped and flat-chested, her skin the green of a lagoon by moonlight. Her hair hung in thick tresses that waved on their own, like seaweed in a current.

The stranger scowled at her. "I have a prior claim, hag."

The woman put a hand to her hip, giving him a glare that mixed anger and contempt. "Hold your tongue, deceiver. She wasn't born in Ravenkirk. Your claim doesn't apply."

"She must choose," said a rustling voice like wind on leaves. "That is the compact."

The third speaker came into view. They were tall and sturdy, with broad shoulders and long, thick limbs. Instead of hair, they wore a crown of autumn leaves, and a fur mantle draped their shoulders. Their face was smooth and featureless, just eyes and a mouth carved into gray bark. Lights like fireflies winked in their eye sockets.

The stranger sneered. "What do I care for your compact? I will not be bound by an agreement that was forced upon me."

"And yet, you are bound," sighed a breathy voice.

The ceiling had disappeared, replaced by the night sky. A silvery moon rose, full and huge. It hung above Victoria, while the others surrounded her in the points of a triangle. She wanted to curl up into a ball, to hide from them. They stared at her with hungry eyes, wanting to carve her up for a feast.

"Victoria is bound by no prior agreement," the moon said. "You may offer her whatever boons you wish, but she must choose."

"Boons?" The stranger snorted. "I offered her a life."

"I can beat that," the sea hag said. "What if she takes too long to decide? Her life spills out by the second."

"Death, too, is a choice," the forest lord said thoughtfully.

"Just so," said the moon. "Make your pleas."

The stranger looked scornfully at the others, then down at Victoria. An emerald-green serpent crawled out of his sleeve. He stroked their head thoughtfully.

"Have I not offered you people enough? Very well, the usual, then. Knowledge of the arts and sciences, weather, oracles, et cetera. I'll still save your life, you're no use to me dead. All in exchange for your service, of course."

"Your gifts are not what they once were, tempter," the sea hag sneered, baring shark's teeth. "Come with *me*, child. I offer you the protection and bounty of the sea. There is power in the deeps, and life. And *transformation*."

A column of water rose from the floor, unfolding into a feminine figure. It danced and shifted next to the sea hag, features transforming from humanoid to piscine and back again—face elongating, eyes becoming bulbous, hair becoming spines and arms becoming tentacles, legs fusing into a long tail.

"Accept your mother's love. Imagine what you could become if you worshipped me."

The forest lord scoffed. "The sea is fickle and ever-changing. Wood *grows*. Wood *waits*. Come to me. I offer the freedom of the wilds."

A wolf padded from the shadows, standing as tall at the shoulder as the forest lord's waist. Their eyes gleamed amber.

"This town, this civilization, all is temporary. Someday it will all be reclaimed. Why not abandon it? What allegiance have you to the world of men?"

Victoria didn't know what to say or who to believe. They towered over her, these gods in the mansion of death, offering her gifts, demanding her service, mediated by the moon. This was too much for her, too strange. She was just a data entry clerk living in a tiny apartment in Boston, not… not whatever they thought she was.

"I don't want this," Victoria said. "I don't want *any* of this."

"Denial of a choice is, itself, a choice," the moon whispered. "Is that, then, your decision?"

"I don't want to die," she sobbed into her hands. "I just want to go home."

A new voice cut through the gloom. It was like smoke and salt air, footsteps echoing over cobblestones and feathered wings in the dark. It caught Victoria's attention as none other had, pulling her head up from between her knees.

"Trying to leave me out of the covenant again?"

An older woman strode out of the shadows. Her dark hair fell around her shoulders like waves, a thin white streaking running from her temple and down the back. She wore a gray blouse the color of slate tiles and a long dark skirt the color of night. Her pointy heeled boots click-clacked on the hardwood floor, silver buttons gleaming in the moonlight. There was something spiky about her, like the exaggerated lines of a cartoon Gothic mansion, and her clothes were shabby and worn. Nonetheless, Victoria trusted this woman immediately.

The tall woman pushed her way into the triangle, the other gods grumbling and shifting to give her space. She knelt in front of Victoria, ignoring their complaints.

"I can't take you home, love, but I can help you make one. I'll offer you something none of them will. Equal partners. You help me and I help you. What do you say?"

That certainly sounded better than what the others demanded, although also like much less than they offered. Maybe that was fair, though. Or maybe she was just having a hard time thinking clearly.

"One condition," Victoria said. Her voice sounded like it was coming from far away, even to her. "You tell me who you are. Who you *really* are."

"Haven't you guessed already?" The tall woman leaned in close, her lips brushing Victoria's ear. *"I'm Ravenkirk."*

As absurd as it was, Victoria knew the truth as soon as she heard it. She threw her arms around the city, catching her in a tight embrace. Why not, at this point? Hadn't she already fallen in love with the town at that first walk around?

"Ravenkirk!" she said. "I choose Ravenkirk!"

The others drew back. The sea hag scowled, like a disappointed mother. The stranger glowered, muttering imprecations under his breath. The forest lord's expression was inscrutable. Ravenkirk kissed Victoria lightly on the forehead. Her lips were pleasantly cool.

"Time to wake up now," she said. "We have a lot to do."

Silvery bells pealed around them, surrounding the moon like an aural halo.

"The covenant is made," it whispered.

11

The moon shone brighter for just a moment. The mansion's walls and floor melted away, replaced by a cobblestone street and the dirty alley. The night sky still hung above her, now blocked out by storm clouds and pelting rain. The water had washed away the pool of blood, and when Victoria put a hand to her side, the wound had already closed.

The tall woman was gone, but Ravenkirk surrounded her. Victoria patted the cobblestones beneath her and could almost swear she felt them tremble in response.

She pushed herself to her feet, dusting off her limbs. She looked around, and Ravenkirk's roads and alleys spread out before her. She could feel Tabitha and Bianca two blocks away, running toward where they thought she was. Nicodemus was three blocks past them, clutching his head in pain and running the wrong direction to find either her or Mercy. Thorn was in an alley on the other side of Main Street; they thought they were stalking Mercy, but it was really the other way around. The traitorous witch was hiding not far away, having left a trail for her former colleague. If Victoria didn't move quickly, hers wouldn't be the only blood spilled tonight.

*Don't worry*, Ravenkirk whispered in her head. *We can do quickly.*

The alleys unfolded for her. Victoria took off running. She turned a corner and emerged in front of Tabitha and Bianca. Bianca's eye widened at the state of her, while Tabitha just looked relieved.

"Victoria! There you are!" She ran up and threw her free arm around Victoria. "We thought Mercy had gotten you."

"It looks like she did." Bianca gestured to the blood staining Victoria's dress.

"Yes and no," Victoria said. "It's kind of complicated and I don't have time to explain. I know where Mercy is; we have to catch her before she hurts someone else."

Bianca bared her bloody teeth in a ferocious snarl. "Where?"

Victoria jerked her thumb over her shoulder. "The other side of Main Street; the alley behind the bookstore."

Tabitha made a face. "Fuck. That whole part of town's a maze; we'll never catch her."

Victoria grabbed their hands. "Don't worry, I know a shortcut."

She began running again, pulling them after her. The alleys unfolded again, blurring as she skipped across them. Victoria understood this was a temporary thing—her needs and

Ravenkirk's aligned at the moment—but reveled in the feeling. For that brief instant, caught in-between the tangled streets with her new friends at her side, she felt completely at home for the first time in years. Her heart hammered in her chest. She wanted to sing.

Then she landed in the alley, Mercy hiding just ahead. The witch was crouched behind a stack of wooden pallets, bloody knife in her hand, waiting for Thorn to follow her trail from the alley's other end. She whirled around when she heard the three sets of boots hit the cobblestones. Eyes wide, Mercy spat a vile curse. Tabitha let go of Victoria's hand and flung her own out, brandishing the protective talisman wrapped around her wrist. The air crackled around them, like a localized lightning storm, and the curse transformed into something hideous with too many teeth. They skittered off into the shadows and disappeared.

"Nice try." Tabitha smirked. "The blessing of St. Magdalen Invicta guards us from your power."

Mercy sneered and brandished her knife. "You pathetic little dabbler. I don't need the craft to kill you."

She started to rise from her crouch. Before she could act, Bianca was on top of her, hand around her throat. Mercy struggled to cry out, but Bianca's grip was too tight. She lashed out, sinking her blade into Bianca's stomach. It stuck fast, but the wound didn't bleed. Bianca looked down at it, unimpressed.

"Tried that. Didn't take."

She raised her pallid fist high, ready to smash Mercy's head in. Suddenly sick at the thought, Victoria cried out for her to stop. Bianca's fist hung in the air, trembling, but she didn't strike. Not, as Victoria had hoped, because she asked her to yield.

"It wasn't her." Bianca's voice was tight as steel cable. "It wasn't her that killed me."

"You're sure?" Tabitha asked.

Bianca whirled around, still holding Mercy by the throat. Her one eye blazed cold blue.

"Of course I'm fucking sure! I can feel the rage in my chest. It's practically the only thing left *to* feel. But not for her. She doesn't owe me her blood."

"Fuck." Tabitha lowered her crossbow but didn't put it away. "What does that mean?"

Despite the hand at her throat, Mercy snickered. "It means she can't kill me. She has no claim on my life."

Bianca cocked her head to one side. "You're sure about that?"

Her grip on Mercy's throat tightened. Mercy gasped, flailing at Bianca's arm to no avail. She kicked at Bianca's fabulous stomach, but Bianca took no notice. By her expression, neither did she take any satisfaction from Mercy's pain, but she didn't relent. Not until Victoria put a hand on her shoulder.

"Don't kill her, Bianca. Please."

Bianca looked over her shoulder, frowning. "She tried to kill you."

"I know. That doesn't mean I want her to die."

"Listen to her," Mercy gasped. *"Please."*

*"Fine."*

Bianca didn't let go of Mercy's throat, but she loosened her grip enough for the witch to breathe. Mercy sucked in a ragged gasp of air, still grabbing onto Bianca's forearm. From the way she glared at Victoria, she wasn't particularly grateful. Victoria noted that with disappointment but little surprise.

"You're fucking welcome, Mercy," she snapped. "And you have something that belongs to me."

Victoria yanked the bag off Mercy's shoulder. The key Wilhelmina had left her was still inside. The little ruby gleamed in the light, winking at her. Victoria retrieved it and thrust the bag back into Mercy's arms.

"So what *do* we do with her?" Tabitha said. "We can't let her run around loose."

"She'll have lost Maledicta's protection," Bianca said. "The rest of the coven may kill her for what she's done."

"If we don't, Nicodemus will," Thorn said, coming around the corner. "The least favorite Ruthven doesn't know the meaning of restraint."

Tabitha stiffened. She didn't raise her crossbow, but her finger lingered near the trigger. Thorn's eyes flicked to the weapon then at their former colleague caught in Bianca's grip. Their expression was unreadable, their hands held out at the ready.

"Thorn," Victoria said with relief. "Mercy was waiting to ambush you."

Thorn nodded once, warily. "So I gathered. What do you intend to do with her?"

"Ladybug doesn't want us killing her." Bianca sounded disappointed. "I assume that extends to you, too."

"You assume correctly." Despite her words, Victoria's hand fell to the closed wound in her side. It didn't sting, but the scar felt cold.

"We can't turn her over to the police." Tabitha made a face. "Beyond the morality of it, Goth knows *what* the sheriff will do."

"Depends on which of the powers that be he's more afraid of now." Thorn fixed Victoria with a stern look. "One way or another, she has to leave Ravenkirk."

"Then she will."

A surge of power swirled within Victoria's breast. She felt the cobblestones beneath her, the brick walls around her, as if they were her own skin. She breathed in and a chill wind rushed up the city's streets. Her thoughts crackled down the power lines. If she turned her head, she thought she'd see Ravenkirk herself standing beneath her, endorsing what she was about to do.

"Mercy Chambers." Victoria's voice hummed with electricity, crashed like waves against the pier. "Ravenkirk rejects you. You are no longer welcome within her borders. Whatever sanctuary you seek, find it elsewhere, for you will have none within Ravenkirk!"

The doom settled heavily on Mercy's shoulders. She jerked and thrashed, as if she was having a seizure. Alarmed, Bianca let her go. She fell to the ground, hard, but didn't stay down long. With a spine-wrenching jerk, she forced herself back upright. Mercy scuttled back, limbs akimbo, moving like a badly puppeted marionette. She screamed in rage but could do nothing but flee the alley. Her voice was soon lost in the night, gradually fading as she left Ravenkirk behind her.

Tabitha stared in the direction she fled, dumbfounded. After a moment of silence, she stammered out, "We tried that with Nicodemus. Didn't take."

"We didn't try *that* with Nicodemus," Thorn said.

Victoria nodded. "This will work. She's no longer welcome within Ravenkirk."

"How did you do that?" Tabitha asked.

Victoria turned to look at the spirit of Ravenkirk. The tall woman no longer stood behind her, but Victoria could still *feel* the city all around her. Ravenkirk was pleased.

"I made another friend." She looked at the others, smiling. "I've made a *lot* of friends. It's been a pretty good day."

Tabitha nodded slowly, disbelieving. "Do you need a change of clothes? Because your dress is ruined."

Victoria glanced down at her clothes. Dark purple or no, the bloodstain covering her from collarbone to knee was obvious, as was the large rent on the left side of her chest. She ran a finger along the rent's edge. It was already starting to fray.

"Shit. Does anyone know how to get bloodstains out of fabric?"

"I do." Bianca pulled Mercy's knife out of her stomach. She snapped the blade off and tossed the pieces into the dumpster. "Come on, Ladybug. Let's get you back to the Abbey."

Bianca took point. Tabitha slid her arm through Victoria's, while Thorn took up the rear. Victoria let them lead her back through the twisting streets to her lodging. She closed her eyes for a moment and smiled, savoring the smell of the autumn air at night, the feel of the cobblestones beneath her feet and Tabitha's warmth against her side.

It was a strange little town, but it was starting to feel like home.

12

"I can't believe it! I can't believe those *bitches* had the nerve to threaten you!"

Belinda stormed through the candle-lit darkness of Mooncroft Manor's cavernous library. Her voice faded in and out as she wove through the stacks. Nicodemus paid her little mind, engrossed as he was in his own studies at a table in the middle of the room, until he heard the smack of her fist against leatherbound tomes.

"Mind the books!" he snapped. "Those are the family treasure, such as it is."

"'Family treasure'! Family *nothing!*" she shouted back. "Those *nobodies* challenged a *Ruthven!* On the street! In front of everyone!"

"In the middle of the night." Nicodemus' voice was mild, like velvet over a blade. "I assure you, my reputation is undamaged."

"*Your* reputation? What about *mine!* Everyone saw us together at the Abbey. They know we're… we're *associated*."

She poked her lip out in a pout, trying to make her wide eyes look innocent and plaintive. Nicodemus didn't look up from the cards spread out in a wide fan on the table, their glossy black and gold backs gleaming in the candlelight. Frustrated, she minced up to the table and leaned against it.

"Nickie, you said you were going to restore the family!" she whined.

"And I intend to do so, *in good time*." He ran a greedy finger over the card backs, suppressing a shiver of hunger. "Frankly, I think you need to learn to appreciate the benefits of being underestimated."

"I've been underestimated *all my life*. I'm sick of it! I want to be more than just a backup! Nickie, you *promised*."

"I did, dear Belle. And I aim to deliver. You just need to be patient."

Nicodemus could swear the cards trembled under his touch, like living things. Margali Harper's personal tarot deck. How Old Lady Bruttenholm had gotten it and not her granddaughter Maledicta, Nicodemus couldn't say, although he was sure *thereby* hung a tale. Nor could he guess why she'd left it to *him*, of all people. The letter she'd left him offered few answers.

Perhaps in her age and senility, the old bat just wanted to burn everything down after her. She'd never trusted him. The feeling had always been mutual. He remembered her eye on him, going back to his childhood. Weighing. Measuring. *Judging*.

Well, she was dead now and he was back home. Whatever

post-mortem agenda she hoped he'd carry out had better align with his own goals. He was working for no one else.

"We're going to do what no one in this town has done in ages, love." Nicodemus drew a card at random. "We're going to play the long game."

It was the Hierophant, the fifth major arcana, but not the image found in any mainstream deck. Margali's deck was custom; she had no truck with the Smith-Ryder-Waite symbolism. Her Hierophant dressed like a 19th Century gentleman, with green eyes and delicate features. An emerald halo radiated from his upraised right hand, fingers extended in the sign of the Evil Eye, and a heavy emerald ring sat on his left hand. A star seal worked in copper hung above his head, like a pentacle but more complex. He recognized the figure instantly. Anyone walking into Mooncroft Manor would.

"What game were *you* playing, Margali?" he whispered to himself.

"Our first step is to find out what happened to the old hag's records," Belinda said, resuming her pacing. "Someone stole those right out from under us! I want their head!"

"All in good time, Belle."

Nicodemus drew another card. It was the two of cups, reversed. Two women held black chalices full of wine, clinking them together in a toast. A leaping fish hung over the woman on the right, a wolf behind the one on the left.

"Our *actual* first step is to gather allies. Auntie Dearest still holds too much sway in Ravenkirk to challenge directly. She has the loyalty of the other families."

He drew a third card. The fifteenth major arcana. It depicted a white-faced figure in a black cloak with bloody hands. In the background, a dark building sat beneath a full moon. Nicodemus was certain it was meant to be Mooncroft Manor itself.

The card fell from suddenly nerveless fingers. Surely that was just a family legend. It couldn't be real. Even with all he knew, he couldn't believe *that*.

Behind him, Belinda said something he didn't hear. He ignored her, sweeping the cards together and returning them to their velvet-lined box. Old Lady Bruttenholm's letter lay open beside his hand, taunting him.

*Nicodemus,*

*I know what you want, and it's everything.*

*You don't care about your family, and you don't care about this town. Fair enough, I suppose. None of them have done much to inspire love in you.*

*I know something you do care about.*

*Enoch is alive, Nicodemus. I won't tell you where he is, but I can promise that if you help Victoria Williams, she will lead you to him.*

*What happens next is up to you, and to her.*

*Warmest Regards,*

*Wilhelmina Bruttenholm*

*P.S. – Don't tell Maledicta you have her grandmother's deck. It won't be worth it.*

The woman they called Bianca Burke stood in front of the sink, staring at the reflection in the mirror. Someone knocked on the door to the shared bathroom. She ignored them. They weren't relevant.

She turned her head back and forth, lifted and lowered her chin, examining every inch of her face. Her cheekbones were high and pronounced, her chin coming to a sharp point. She supposed it might have once been considered "heart-shaped", before her cheeks sunk in. Her pale blonde hair, once tied in a tight bun, hung in thin, limp mess. Her skin was pale and tinged with blue, her once-full lips chapped. She drew them back, baring her teeth. They looked long. Perhaps that was her dry gums retreating.

One eye, piercing blue, rolled in its socket, still bloodshot. The other hid behind a dirty bandage. Or at least, it should have. She knew the eye was gone, recognized that from the narrowed field of view and the dried rivulets of blood running down the left side of her face. She took a deep breath, more out of habit than need, and ripped the bandage off. She thought it should have hurt, from the way it pulled at her skin, but she felt nothing.

The person outside knocked again, asking if anyone was inside. She didn't respond.

A gaping hole stared back. The flesh around the empty socket was crusty with dried blood, but it looked smooth. Whatever had plucked the eye out had been efficient. She supposed she felt grateful for that.

Gingerly, she placed her finger just under her eyelid. She couldn't see it now, though she felt the pressure of her fingertip. She could feel something, at least.

She slipped the finger up and into the socket, waiting for her body to react. Nothing.

She laughed, a raspy noise that sounded more like a chain-smoker's cough.

There was a third knock. Now whoever it was called Bianca's name, asking after her health. They warned they were about to unlock the door.

Bianca. The name meant nothing to her. It rattled around the emptiness inside her, finding no connection. She didn't remember who Bianca was or what had brought her to Ravenkirk. She didn't remember anything but a handful of names and faces, none of them hers. They were… friends? Enemies? Targets? She would have to sort that out if she was to keep going.

A key rattled in the door's lock. The door swung open, revealing a tall femme with long purple braids. They held a box and an envelope in their black-fingernailed hands. An expression of concern crossed their face. The pale woman reached for a name and found it. Thorn Hale. They worked at the Abbey, where the pale woman was staying.

"Bianca. We need to talk," Thorn said.

The pale woman turned to look at them, blood-stained hands hanging loosely at her side. Bianca. She supposed she might as well be Bianca. That name came with obligations, but she already had some to the woman on the third floor. Victoria Williams. She had to protect her.

She had to protect Victoria and kill whoever did this to her.

"So, talk," Bianca said.

Thorn didn't relax. Their eyes flicked up and down, taking Bianca's measure. The pale woman made them uncomfortable. Well, that was fair. Bianca didn't know much, but she understood that her bloodstained clothes, her gaping empty eye socket, and the open gash in her throat were something of a sight.

"It's a little against the rules, but I figure you're a lot past that now." Thorn offered Bianca the box and envelope. "Mistress Bruttenholm left you something, too. We thought it was an oversight, but…"

They shrugged. Bianca said nothing. She just stared at Thorn for a moment. Then she accepted the offered items, if only to make Thorn go away.

"That's it, then," Thorn said, clearly uncomfortable. They turned to leave, then looked back over their shoulder. "There's one more thing. A little sum of money. Enough to keep your room paid up for the foreseeable."

"I don't need a room," Bianca said.

"You at least need somewhere to keep a change of clothes and shower," Thorn said. "You look like shit."

Bianca turned back to the mirror. She supposed she did, in fact, look like shit. That might make her job harder. She was going to stand out enough as it was. No need to have everyone who saw her calling the police. She'd shower later.

She set the box on the sink and opened the envelope. It held a simple letter, written in a spidery hand. The name at the bottom meant no more to her than the name at the top, but the instructions fired something deep in her breast. Something almost like a heartbeat.

> *Ms. Burke,*
>
> *Thank you for completing your assignment. Your professionalism is, as promised, beyond reproach. With that in mind, I am afraid I must contract you for another.*
>
> *As long as she is in Ravenkirk, Victoria Williams is in danger. I can't predict how many enemies she will have, but they will be drawn from the most powerful families. The Talbots, the Gilmans, and of course the Ruthvens. The others will seek to subvert her. Dolores will simply want to kill her.*
>
> *If I've guessed right, you will have no problem following this request. In fact, I suspect you'll be able to think of little else. I'm truly sorry for that. It couldn't be helped.*
>
> *I can't fix this for you. I doubt any power under Heaven can. All I can do is make things a little easier.*
>
> *Keep Victoria safe, Ms. Burke. Do that and you will eventually find peace. Don't, and you'll likely haunt my town forever. Neither of us wants that.*
>
> *With Deepest Sympathies,*
> *Wilhelmina Bruttenholm*

Something hot lanced through Bianca's breast. For the briefest second, heat washed over her face. Her vision went red.

When it returned, she stared at an array of cracks spiderwebbing across the bathroom mirror. The letter was crumpled in her pale fists. Shards of glass stuck bloodlessly in her knuckles. She picked them out one by one, dropping them in the metal bin next to the toilet. She almost tossed the letter in after them but thought better of it. That would be poor operational security. She might not know who she was, but she knew that wasn't like her. Instead, she stuck it in her back pocket.

The wooden box waited on the sink. The symbol engraved in the lid sparked something like a memory. She recognized it as Wilhelmina's seal. She'd seen that before, somewhere. She couldn't trust it, exactly, but it still centered her.

She lifted the lid. Sitting on a purple cushion in the middle of the velvet box was a glass eye, pale white with an emerald-green iris. She held it up between two fingers. The glass was cool even to her own touch.

"I don't know who you were, Wilhelmina Bruttenholm." Her raspy voice echoed in the small bathroom. "But you were a complete bitch."

She turned the glass eye around and popped it into her open socket. She rolled her eyes, letting it settle. She blinked twice and was shocked to see binocular vision had returned.

"Well. This is going to be interesting."


Mercy huddled beneath a tree, three hundred feet from Ravenkirk's loose city limits. She'd tried going back. She'd run, she'd crawled, she'd snuck down side roads and hidden paths, hoping to find some way home. It didn't work. Every time she got within ten feet of the town border, her muscles seized up. She couldn't move so much as a finger in the direction of Ravenkirk. Only when she gave up and slunk away was she able to move again.

She'd tried hitching a ride, but the hour was too late. No one was coming. There had been cars earlier, but none that would stop for her. She supposed she must look a fright. She'd been out here for two days now, sleeping in bushes and eating whatever she could scrounge.

The little bitch was going to pay. Everyone was going to pay.

Once she'd hurled herself at the town line so hard she'd wrenched something in her back. Now the muscles screamed at her. She'd tried to ignore the pain, hoping it would pass, but now it was too much. Tears cut lines in the grime on her cheeks, betraying her misery.

She was down to her final option. With her last bit of strength, she'd dragged a fallen log across the road into town. That had probably hurt her back more than anything else, but she didn't care. Someone was going to stop now. The market would be opening soon; farmers driving in with their wares. When they stopped to clear the road, she could sneak into the bed of their truck. They'd throw her out the second they saw her, but she didn't care. Not as long as she got back into town.

The growl of a heavy engine cut through her sulking. For a moment, her hopes rose. It was going to work! She was going home!

Then the headlights came from the wrong direction. The battered truck was leaving town, not coming in!

The truck rolled to a stop. The door opened and a trio of bearded men in weathered denim and flannel hopped out. The Yonders. Her heart sank. She couldn't imagine a less helpful bunch.

The two big men went to move the log while their leader stood and watched. She told herself this was fine. She'd just wait and move the blockade back once they were on the road to their compound. She winced at a sudden twinge of pain. *If* she could still move it.

Their leader, Waylon, jerked his head her way. She hunkered down, hoping she was still hidden in the withered brush. His bright eyes ran over the brush, but she didn't think he could see her. Then he lifted his head in the air and sniffed, like a dog.

Beneath his wiry beard, he broke out in a wide grin.

"Mercy Chambers!" he called. "There you are!"

She crept back, trying to bury herself deeper. It was no use. He tromped forward, coming right at her. Before she could run, he reached down and grabbed her arm, pulling her out of her hiding place. A spasm of pain wracked her back, and she cried out. Waylon paid her agony no heed. He grabbed her jaw, holding her firmly but not painfully.

"Look what we have here, boys!" he called over his shoulder. "It's Miss Harper's little lost lamb!"

The two big men—Jon and Eric—threw the log to the side of the road. They stood next to it, staring at Waylon and Mercy, waiting to see what happened next. What Waylon decided.

"I'm not lost," Mercy said through chattering teeth.

"No? Out here all on your lonesome? Hiding in a ditch like a scared skunk?"

She didn't know how to respond to that. She stared into his eyes. They were pale, like ice chips. Something danced within them, a light she used to think she saw in Maledicta's eyes.

"Do you know what they're saying in town, little Mercy?" He stroked her cheek with his rough thumb. "They're saying Miss Harper threw you out. They're saying you're an outcast."

Tears welled in her eyes. That couldn't be true. She'd done what Maledicta had asked. Okay, maybe she'd done a little more than that, but it was all for her. All for the Abbey!

Honest.

"You're lying," she said, but her voice wavered.

"I wish I was, little Mercy."

Waylon let her go. He put a gentle hand on her back, right where the muscles jumped and screamed. She gasped, but the pain went away. Waylon bent down and whispered in her ear.

"It's okay. We're outcasts too."

Straightening, Waylon called out to his followers. "In the truck, boys. We've got to get back. Call home and tell 'em there's another one joining us for breakfast."

Mercy didn't say anything as Waylon led her to the truck. Eric climbed in before her, then Jon helped her up. She sat between the two big men, feeling warm and safe for the first time in two days.

She was going home.

*Read on for a sample chapter of the next in the series:*

# SHADOWS OVER
# RAVENKIRK

## 2: CIVIL BLOOD AND CIVIL HANDS

01

From across the country they came. In twos and threes, by car and by train, they came. Some came out of curiosity, some out of anger, some lusting for wealth or power or revenge, but all out of loyalty. Nicodemus Ruthven called for his family to attend him at their ancestral seat, and slowly but surely his family answered.

Generations of Ruthvens had spread across the continent, down the Eastern Seaboard and across the plains to the Southwest and West Coast and even to Alaska. Many had taken on new names over the years through marriage or adoption or deceit. They were Griffins now, or Essexes, or Hyde-Ruthvens or Ruthven-Myers, but they were all Ruthvens, and Ravenkirk was their home. After long years, the little town on the seashore was welcoming its flock back to the nest.

Once, Mooncroft Manor had been their redoubt. The rambling mansion on the high hill had hosted a veritable army of relations, some permanently, the rest a rotating cast of fosters and visitors. Over the decades, as the family scattered and their fortunes withered, it had fallen into decay. By the time Nicodemus returned to Ravenkirk, it was a ruin. Now, two weeks after he put out his summons, it still sulked in disrepair, but lights shone in its tall narrow windows, and if they were mostly candlelight, so much the better. The groundskeeper had hacked away at the jungle of the front lawn. Practically an acre of fresh-laid gravel outside the rickety wrought-iron fence supported a small fleet of expensive, eclectic cars. The door, long locked, stood open, and the guardian of the threshold did not bar their entry.

The manor's great dining hall could host dozens. Tonight, it boasted only nineteen, seated at a single long table. They regarded each other warily; they were united by ties of blood, but divided by generations of tangled, inherited feuds. Some looked around the decayed hall with critical eyes, appraising the likely value of the Ruthven's collective fortune and dividing it by the number of relations here. Others contemplated the likely state of the family library, much more valuable to the discerning scholar, and wondered how willing their cousins would be to share. Three, the most cunning and least trusting, kept their eyes on the skinny man at the head of the table. Nicodemus Ruthven slouched in the master's chair, fingers steepled and elbows propped up on the table, and grinned at his family.

His habitual sneer hid his frustration at the state of things. Barely half of the relations he'd invited had come, and only a third of those who truly mattered. He could see by their faces that they were less than impressed, which galled him beyond all reason. True, the house was in a state. Cobwebs choked every corner, the wallpaper was peeling, the fixtures falling off the wall. The service was likewise unworthy. The table ought to be laden with a fine feast instead of six extra-large pizzas from the Flying Saucer Pizzeria off Main Street. The mascot waving from the boxes, a beady-eyed green blob in a spaceship, hardly set the right mood.

Well, it wasn't as if the manor had staff yet. They were making do. At least they had good wine, thank the powers. The ancient wine cellar was intact. He'd fetched up a dozen bottles of fine red himself. In an additional stroke of luck, he was spared the indignity of serving it personally. One of his better cousins had generously provided a servant.

The gray-skinned fellow loomed over him, thick limbs gangling from his ill-fitting suit. The servant didn't turn his yellow eyes to Nicodemus, but filled his glass unerringly. Nicodemus raised the glass to his cousin, only half-mocking.

"Thanks again for the loan of your man, cuz," Nicodemus said. "It's so hard to find good help these days."

Henry Essex, his skinny frame hidden behind a white lab coat, slung one arm over the back of his chair. Smirking, he raised his own glass in salute. His dirty blond hair stuck up like a bottle-brush, held back by heavy goggles on a thick leather strap.

"It's easier if you make them yourself."

The servant lumbered down the table, refilling drinks. The stitches around his cranium peeked out through his stringy black hair. Uncomfortable laughter rippled around the table. Nicodemus' smile flickered in contempt. As if any of his relations were in any position to judge. Look at Nathaniel Hyde-Ruthven there, tearing into a slice of pizza with meticulously sharpened teeth. Or Lobelia Ruthven-Myers, star and sole survivor of a series of grotesque underground films. Not to mention Sam Griffin, whose chemical concoctions were frequently literally mind-melting, or Mormo Ruthven, who'd somehow kept the family name despite a series of late husbands.

Mormo took a long drink of wine. Smacking her lips in satisfaction, she held out her glass for a refill. Her pet Drakaina, a twelve-foot python of no species found in any zoology text, rested across her shoulder. The snake lifted her green head, forked tongue tasting the air.

"A fine vintage, Nicodemus." Her voice was like envenomed smoke. "The 1897, if I'm not mistaken?"

"95." Sam sipped their own glass daintily, raising their narrow nose with the haughtiness of a connoisseur. "The notes of Talbot give it away."

"1895." Tessa Hyde-Ruthven nodded in grotesque approval, thumbing through a well-worn leather-bound book. The Ruthven family crest was embossed on its cover. "The year of the Sinclair Farm Massacre."

Sam rolled their eyes. "I know how the wine is made, Tess."

"We *all* know," Nicodemus said graciously.

Maine lacked the climate for grapes, but like all well-bred families, the Ruthvens had a taste for wine. An *eccentric* taste.

The California branch of the Ruthven-Myers ran a vineyard. The rest of the family contributed as best they could. The discerning palate appreciated the result.

The sulky teenager sitting to Nicodemus' right pouted, her pale blonde hair falling across her face. "*I* don't."

The cousins looked at each other and tittered. The teenager's sulk deepened. She folded her arms and sulked, glaring at the others as if imagining knives plunging into their flesh.

"It's all right, pet." Nicodemus patted her arm, then pushed her wine glass closer. "There's plenty of time to learn the family history."

Tessa turned to her, eyes gleaming. "I'll teach you."

Sam scowled, candlelight glinting off their shorn scalp. "Why doesn't she know the family history? Who is this?"

Lobelia smirked. "Did Nickie bring his latest bit of fun to a *family meeting?*"

The teenager jerked upright, as if she'd been slapped. Nicodemus' smirk fell into a scowl. He leveled his emerald-eyed glare at his cousin. Lobelia tried to glare back, but she couldn't match the heat of Nicodemus' quiet affront. She dropped her eyes, slinking back against her chair and turning her head away. The anger didn't leave Nicodemus' eyes, but his smile returned, lizard-quick.

"None of you have met our youngest cousin, Belinda Pickman-*Ruthven*," Nicodemus said, putting particular stress on her second family name. "I fear our dear auntie has kept her rather sequestered from the rest of the family."

"I can see why." Lobelia dared to lift her head. "A *Pickman*?"

Nicodemus and Belinda both bristled, but it was Mormo who snapped, "That's rich coming from a Ruthven-Myers."

Shouts rang across the room. Tessa leapt to her feet, slamming her family history against the table.

"We agreed!" she shouted. "No shaming family names!"

"Quite right!" Henry wagged a rubber-gloved finger. "Blood is blood."

Mormo stroked Drakaina, unbothered. "Lobelia started it."

"And I'm finishing it." Nicodemus looked around the table sternly. "We're *all* Ruthvens here."

So to speak. Henry was right, to a point; the blood *did* matter, to those skilled in the arts, but it wasn't what made a Ruthven. It was an attitude, and appetite, and most importantly, a strength of will. Nicodemus had it. So did Aunt Delores, he had to admit. Belinda had it, unlike all but a handful of these so-called relatives. Them, he could rely on. The rest, well, they were just numbers.

But he needed numbers.

Nathaniel pounded his meaty fists on the table, rattling the wine glasses. "Enough talk! What are we doing here?!"

Nicodemus favored his brutish cousin with a vulpine smile. "Delicately put as always, cuz."

He unfolded his spindly legs and sprang to his feet. Nicodemus held himself up by his fingertips as he looked down the table, measuring their expressions carefully. They looked at him with curiosity leavened with no small measure of contempt.

So be it. He could work with that.

"I'm sure Nathaniel speaks for all of you. Why have I called you here? It couldn't just be for the pleasure of your company."

"I'm more wondering why you asked us to meet *here*." Tessa smiled sweetly. "Last I'd heard, you were *persona non grata* in Ravenkirk."

Sam leaned in, propping their chin on their fist. "Some trouble with the Gilmans, wasn't it, Tess?"

Mormo frowned mockingly, making a *tsk* sound. *"New money."*

Nicodemus' smile faltered, but didn't drop. He'd expected this. He spread his hands wide, shrugging. As if he was the victim of circumstances beyond anyone's control.

"An unfortunate turn of events," he said, "but the situation has changed. Dare I say, potentially in our favor."

Nathaniel thumped the table again. "Out with it, man!"

Nicodemus leaned closer, as if imparting a terrible secret. "Wilhelmina Bruttenholm is dead."

About half the cousins nodded sagely. The other half erupted into a hubbub, calls of "How?" and "When?" bounding over one another. Evidently the news hadn't traveled west of the Mississippi yet, except to him.

"The 'when' was about a month ago. As to the 'how' …" Nicodemus showed his empty hands, the picture of innocence. "*I* had nothing to do with it."

"Don't be clever, Nickie, it's unattractive," Mormo said.

"I can't help but be clever, Mormo dear." Nicodemus dropped

back into his chair, kicking one leg up casually. "*And* I'm telling the truth. Wasn't me. Wasn't *anyone*, actually. Natural causes, if you can believe it."

Henry scoffed. "I certainly don't."

"I can't blame you. *I* didn't when I heard it, but obviously I wasn't in town." Nicodemus tossed his chin toward their youngest cousin. "Belinda knows the score."

Belinda smiled prettily at the cousins, though her eyes still danced with phantom knives. She sat up straight, smoothing out her green skirt. When she spoke, it was with her best Collinswood Academy diction.

"Mistress Bruttenholm was found in her study on the morning of September third." Belinda tossed her white-gold tresses. "The death was reported by one of her disreputable adventurers. There was no sign of struggle nor of foul play. The coroner determined that the cause of death was likely heart failure. She *was* a very *old* woman."

Henry steepled his rubber-clad fingers. "And who is the coroner working for this week?"

"You asking for information or looking to put in a competing bid?" Nicodemus snickered. "I think it's an honest report, cuz. No one's claimed responsibility and Tabitha Swann hasn't declared a blood feud on anyone."

"*Yet,*" Nathaniel said dourly.

"Well, the night is young!" Nicodemus drummed his fingers against his thigh, self-satisfied. "As I said, the situation is ripe with opportunity."

Tessa looked thoughtful. "With Wilhelmina Bruttenholm off the board, the other families are too busy jostling for position to enforce your exile." She shook her head, dark curls bouncing. "No. It must be more than that. You don't love Ravenkirk that much."

"I *am* quite well set-up in San Francisco," Nicodemus agreed. "It's not about Ravenkirk. It's about the family."

"The family *is* Ravenkirk," Belinda said.

A wave of grumbles washed up the table. The distant cousins took umbrage with the central family's claim of primacy. They always had. Nicodemus raised his hands to quell the insurrection.

"Cousins, cousins. Belinda isn't wrong. Ravenkirk is the home of the Ruthvens. *All* the Ruthvens. The branches of our family tree might be spread wide, but our *roots* are sunk deep in Ravenkirk soil."

Despite themselves, the cousins nodded. In truth, there *was* something about the town that spoke to them, that sang in their blood. Each of them, even those who had never before stepped foot in Ravenkirk, felt a sense of homecoming when they entered the town. The place belonged to them, and they to it.

"*Ravenkirk.*" Tessa relished the sound. "The Ruthven family's first true home since our exile."

"Exactly." Nicodemus smiled. He knew he had them. "Old Graeham Ruthven brought a power across the sea with him. He planted it here. We flourished *here* until some old fools let the family's power wither."

Mormo smiled mirthlessly, revealing long, sharp canines.

"You're going to challenge Dolores."

Lobelia snorted. "That's suicide."

"*Hardly.*" Belinda turned up her sharp nose. "Auntie D's a shadow of her former self."

"I couldn't have put it better myself, Belle." Nicodemus put his hand over hers. "It's not about Aunt Dolores, cousins. It's not about our squabbles with the other families. It's not even about Ravenkirk. We were born to do more than struggle for primacy over one little fishing village. The power that Grandfather Graeham claimed is still buried here. I aim to unearth it."

Nicodemus stood, raising his glass to his family. "Help me, cousins. Take part in our family's restoration, and share in the rewards."

Belinda leapt to her feet, holding her glass high. He smiled graciously at her. It was almost as if she'd been coached.

The other cousins looked back and forth, as if they were trying to see who else was willing to throw their lot in with Nicodemus. For a moment, he feared he'd misjudged the moment. His entire plan threatened to fall apart.

Then Henry rose, lifting his glass. "For the family."

Quiet Annie was next. She held up her wine, one corner of her mouth quirked up. "For Ravenkirk."

Mormo slid from her seat, draining her glass before holding it high. "For old wizard Graeham and his power."

One by one, the rest of the cousins stood. They held their glasses high. Some did it eagerly, others fearing the judgement of their peers, but all of them stood together. Stood with

Nicodemus. His withered heart fluttered in his breast. He nearly laughed in excitement.

"Then let's begin."

*Acknowledgements*

After five years of writing almost exclusively in Amelia Temple's voice, it has been a pleasure to branch out to something completely different. I'll always love my terrible monster gal, but I'm thrilled to play with stories utterly unlike her adventures. There's so much mystery swirling around Victoria Williams and her new friends, allies, and enemies, and I can't wait to explore it with you.

As ever, my greatest supporter continues to be my beloved wife and best friend, Frankie Valentine. Every idea I throw at her, no matter how strange, she encourages me to follow up on. If I seem to write quickly, it's because I can't wait for her to see the next part.

My found family, Ryan and Johanna, are always my dearest friends and biggest fans. Thank you so much for your continued kindness and encouragement.

Thanks as well to the queer indie publishing cult. Where other writers treat one another as rivals and sources of drama, these amazing weirdos try to lift one another up and celebrate one anothers' successes. Abra, Ever, Lea, Quill, Mel, Shimaira, Sadhbh, Sara, SE, Kara, also Kara—you're terrific and I'm happy to be your friends. I hope we can meet in person someday!

There aren't many publishers who will pick up a ten-book horror novella serial off just the first book. Narielle Living has done it twice now. I'm so grateful she believes in my work enough to commit to this project with me.

As always, thank you, you beautiful disaster, for reading along with me.

Be seeing you!

Vivian Moira Valentine is a rad trans lady who loves monsters. When she was a child, she found the Crestwood House Monster Series at her local library and it's all been downhill from there. Now everything she likes is horrible. When not writing, Vivi enjoys card and board games and plotting out more tabletop RPG campaigns than she will ever have time to run. Vivi lives in Virginia Beach with her amazing wife Frankie and their son, as well as an ever-growing collection of action figures. She is the author of The Amelia Temple Series, and her short fiction has appeared in a number of publications.

To find work by Viivan Moira Valentine, follow her on social media, or support her writing on Patreon, scan the QR code below!